I KNOW

by

Stephen Bratcher

WillMarie Publishing
Phone: 615-461-5739
Email: WillMariePublishing@gmail.com

Publisher: WillMarie Publishing
IG&FB: WillMariePublishing
Cover Design: Marcus Levar Powell
IG: MarcoLevar_Graphix_N_Arts

Inspired by the short story "I Know" written by Stephen Bratcher and Markus Boyd

Library of Congress Registration Number: TXu002288662

Introduction

In Hazleton United States Penitentiary in April 2020, two inmates, Slim and Trey, are sitting in their cell. Slim is writing in a notebook while Trey is telling a story about what happened in the cafeteria yesterday. Sensing that Slim isn't paying any attention to him, Trey asks, "Slim what the hell you are doing mane?" Slim says, "Working on this movie script. Me and my homeboy are trying to put together a movie. He sends me what he writes, and I send him what I write and he's gonna try to get it in the hands of some of them big time Hollywood movie execs." A laughing Trey says, "Mane who the hell you think you are, Bike Lee? No, you must be Dumb Singleton. I got it; you're Martin Fugazzi or Quentin Tortino's Pizza. Mane get the hell out of here with all that daydreaming. Next you gonna be telling me about Slim's Boom Boom Room." As Trey continues to talk, Slim begins to read what he has written to himself. "We as poor folk have always had to go through some of the most difficult of trials and tribulations. Most of us just maintain or overcome them while some of us just get stuck in them or take drastic measures to attempt to find a way out. Now before you say things can't be that bad, imagine looking through our eyes and you would view the world from a very different perspective. You will see mothers and fathers doing whatever it takes to provide for their families and young men selling drugs just to get by. And if you ever get a chance to encounter one of these people and ask them, "Do you know what you are doing is wrong?", they will give you the simplest response, which is, "I Know". By them answering "I Know" shows that they not only know what they are doing is wrong, but that they also have the potential to do right when presented with opportunities. I know you are probably reading this saying, "You mean to tell me there are people that are willing to risk their life and freedom by participating in criminal activity when they know what it will eventually lead to?" The answer is Yes. Not that I'm condoning what they do, but sometimes you have to know where a person comes from to fully understand why they are where they are at in life. This is the story of three individuals who are faced with dire circumstances that eventually lead them to travel roads that they otherwise would have never traveled."

Chapter 1
Good Girl Gone Bad?

Chapter 1 – Good Girl Gone Bad?

It is a beautiful spring morning with the sunshine peeking through the blinds of the home of Terry and Stacy Jackson. The alarm on Terry's cellphone goes off and he angrily rolls over and hits the snooze button. He gets up, uses the restroom and then heads outside to get the newspaper. He comes back in and heads to the kitchen to throw the plastic bag that was around the paper into the garbage. As he looks in the garbage can, he sees an open envelope addressed to him and Stacy. He opens the envelope and discovers that it is an invitation to Stacy's family reunion. He heads back to the bedroom and angrily says, "Hey baby, why didn't you tell me about your family reunion? I would like to meet some people in your family." Stacy says, "To be honest with you, I wasn't planning on going. My family is very embarrassing, and I would rather you not meet them. They are, how can I say this? Ummm.. Ghetto." Terry yells, "What? Your family can't be that bad. Mane I'm from South Memphis ain't nothing your family can do that I haven't seen before." Stacy says, "You just don't understand." Terry yells back, "I understand alright, you think you're better than them. Don't forget where I'm from and how I used to be. I'm out of here. I'm about to go walk this dog and get ready for work. Can you fix me some breakfast please your royal highness?"

Terry leaves the house to take their dog Mimi out for her normal morning walk. Terry mumbles to himself, "The nerve of

Chapter 1 – Good Girl Gone Bad?

her stuck-up ass calling somebody ghetto. I swear if she wasn't my wife, I would knock her ass out." About ten minutes into his walk, he notices a very attractive young woman standing on the corner. Terry says to the woman, "Good morning, how are you doing today." She replies, "I'm doing fine. How about yourself? You lookin' for a good time?" A surprised Terry says, "Excuse me." She says, "Are you deaf or something? Are you looking for a good time? Terry says, "Man I heard you, but I just didn't think y'all worked this early. Y'all need a union or something. You might want to talk to your manager about a shift change because you might not get that much business during this time of day or in this neighborhood." She yells at Terry, "Look I'm just trying to make a couple of dollars man. I don't need your dry ass sense of humor." Terry responds by saying, "Ok I tell you what, I'll just give you these fifty dollars. I don't want anything in return, but you might want to consider a career change because this ain't no way for a woman to live and it's obvious that you aren't good at this prostitution thing." As she rocks back and forth, she says, "You think I don't know that? Here, take your damn money back. I don't need your charity. You don't know a damn thing about me." Terry says, "You're right, you're right. I don't know anything about you. I just don't like to see my people out here like this. Keep the money. I'm sorry about that and you have a good day." As Terry walks off, she sits down on the curb and says to herself, "I know, you're right, but if you only knew what I've been through."

Fifteen years earlier in Teresa Tonechia Robinson's childhood home, a thirteen-year-old Teresa listens as her mother and father argue. "Look, I'm tired of this shit. You're getting on my damn nerves always accusing me of doing something", says Teresa's father. Teresa's father, Jesse Robinson, is a tall skinny dark-skinned man with long dreadlocked hair and four gold teeth in his mouth. He works as a mechanic at a small automotive shop. He is a great father, but he is also a womanizer that seems to always get caught by Teresa's mother. "Hell, I wouldn't always accuse you of something if you weren't always doing something you ain't got no business doing", Teresa's mother replies. Teresa's mother, Fay, is a very outspoken, short, heavy set, thirty-year-old woman. She is a beautician at a local beauty salon. She and Jesse were childhood sweethearts that have been married for ten years. Jesse screams, "I told you those women are lying on me." "Whatever you lying bastard", screams Fay. "To hell with you then, I'm out of here", yells Jesse. He grabs a few items, hugs Teresa, gives her a kiss and tells her he loves her and leaves. This would be one of the many things that would forever change Teresa's life.

A couple of months later, after returning home from her weekly visit with her father, Teresa opens the door to her house

Chapter 1 – Good Girl Gone Bad?

and is greeted by a tall bald man sitting on the couch wearing nothing but a wife beater and boxers. "Hi, you must be Teresa, says the man. I've heard a lot about you. I've been dying to meet you. I'm Fay's, I mean, your mother's new man. I'm James and I'm going to be living here for a while. You are as pretty as your mother said you were. Come over here and sit down and talk to me." James is a small-time drug dealer that Teresa's mom grew up with. Teresa says, "Where is my mom?" James says, "She just left to go to the store, but will be back shortly." Teresa says to James, "It was nice to meet you, but I have to go now; I have homework to do." Teresa runs to her bedroom and immediately locks the door. Teresa sits with her back pressed against her bedroom door listening to music and doing her math homework. James knocks on the door a few times asking Teresa if she needs help with her homework. Each time Teresa declines his offer. Teresa calls her favorite cousin Pumpkin and tells her what's going on. Pumpkin is fifteen years old and lives with their grandmother since her parents died in a car wreck. Teresa asks Pumpkin if she can stay on the phone with her until her mother gets home. They talk for a while about school and boys until Pumpkin has to get off the phone so she can go to the store for their grandmother.

After about an hour, Teresa's mother finally arrives home. Fay screams, "Teresa why is that damn door closed? You

Chapter 1 – Good Girl Gone Bad?

know you can't be keeping that door closed. Now come out here and help put these groceries up." Teresa responds by saying, "Yes ma'am I will, but can you come help me with this last math problem first?" Fay walks into Teresa's room and says, "Let me see the damn problem. Hurry up. And since when did you need help from me with homework Ms. 4.0 Grade Point Average?" Teresa whispers, "Who is that man and why is he here? He creeps me out." "That man is my business, now you get in there and put those groceries up. By the way, did your jail bird older brother happen to call while I was out?" says Fay. Teresa says, "No Ma'am. And do you have to always call him a jailbird? You know he didn't do anything." As Teresa puts away the groceries, James comes in the kitchen, still wearing nothing but a wife beater and boxers, and offers to help Teresa. As Teresa struggles to put a can of peas on the top shelf of the cabinet, James gets behind her and takes the can out of her hand and places it on the shelf. Teresa asks if he can finish putting the groceries away and runs back to her room. She puts her headphones on, and eventually falls asleep listening to music. About an hour goes by, and Teresa is awakened by her mother screaming. She jumps up, and as she makes her way down the hall the screaming stops and she hears James say, "Now get up and fix me some dinner." When she realizes what's going on, she turns to run back to her room and James emerges from the room completely naked and

Chapter 1 – Good Girl Gone Bad?

calls Teresa's name. When she turns around, he winks at her and walks into the bathroom. Teresa stays in her bedroom until her mother lets her know that dinner is ready.

With James in the house and having to leave her bedroom door open, Teresa could barely sleep. She finally falls asleep at 3 am only to be awaken by James, which seems like minutes later, asking her if she had to go to school. She jumps up frightened not realizing that it was already 6:30 and her bus comes at 7:15. Teresa takes a quick shower then spends ten minutes deciding on what to wear although she only has two pair of shoes and a few skirts, a couple pairs of jeans and a few shirts. After getting dressed, she grabs an apple and runs to the bus stop. The other kids are already there waiting on the bus. They immediately begin to make jokes about her outfit. Teresa was in such a hurry that she didn't realize that she actually put on the same clothes that she had on the previous day. The bus pulls up as she was getting ready to head back home to change so she just boards the bus with the rest of the kids. They continue to poke fun at her the entire bus ride to school. As she exits the bus, some of the other girls join in and begin talking about Teresa also. Pumpkin sees what's going on and gives Teresa the sweater that she was wearing over her dress shirt. "Here, put this on, she says. Don't listen to them cuz." Although she now has a sweater on hiding the shirt she had on the previous day, some of the kids continue

Chapter 1 – Good Girl Gone Bad?

to poke fun at her throughout the day. While on the way to lunch Teresa even goes and tells the principal what the other kids have been doing all day. The principal tells her to suck it up and just go to lunch. After getting her lunch, she finds Pumpkin and sits next to her. Teresa says, "I'm gonna beat the mess out of the next one of these lil girls that says something about me." Pumpkin says, "Please don't do that cuz, you will get kicked out of school." Just as Pumpkin was finishing her sentence, one girl throws a fry at Teresa and calls her stinky. Teresa immediately stands up and grabs the girl by her hair and starts punching her in the face. The girl falls to the ground and Teresa continues to punch and kick her. The school officer eventually comes over and pulls Teresa away and takes her to the principal's office. The principal immediately suspends Teresa for two days. Teresa pleads with the principal, but he just tells her to call her mother. He says, "I don't know what has gotten into you today. You are normally so well behaved. Hopefully this suspension will help you get your mind right." Teresa knows that her mom will be upset that she got suspended, but even more upset if she has to leave work to get her, so Teresa picks up the phone and only pretends to call her mom. Teresa says to the principal, "Sir, my mom says she will be here in about fifteen minutes." The principal tells the school officer to wait with Teresa until her mother shows up. However, right after the principal leaves, the

Chapter 1 – Good Girl Gone Bad?

officer gets a call regarding a fight, so he leaves the office and tells Teresa not to go anywhere. But as soon as the officer leaves, Teresa runs out of the office and leaves the building.

As Teresa walks home, she cries thinking about how she is going to tell her mother that she's been suspended from school. After walking about ten minutes, a large black Cadillac pulls up beside her. One man gets out the car and walks up the street while another man in the car says, "Hey girl, where are you headed?" Teresa ignores the man and just keeps walking. The man finally says, "It's me, James. Come on and get in the car and let me give you a ride home." Teresa says, "No thanks, I can walk." "Ok, it's all good, says James. I just hope the police don't see you walking home at this time of day and lock your lil ass up for truancy. Hopefully I will see you at the crib tonight if you aren't in juvenile." As James starts to pull off Teresa runs to the car and tells him that she changes her mind and that she wants a ride. Teresa gets in and notices a gun in James' lap along with a wad of money and a fairly large bag of marijuana. He places the items under his seat and drives off. James turns the radio down and says, "So why ain't your bad ass in school? You must be skipping to meet up with some lil boy?" A shocked Teresa immediately says, "No. I got suspended for two days for fighting. I don't know how I'm going to tell my mom about this. She is going to kill me." James says to Teresa, "Maybe she doesn't have to find out. I can sign whatever needs to be signed and you can hang out with me while I work for the next two days." Teresa responds by saying, "I guess that's ok. Thanks. Where do you work anyway?" "I'm my own boss, says James. I sell the stuff I just put under my seat any and everywhere to whoever wants it. That's enough about what I do. Why in the hell were you fighting?" Teresa says, "The girls at school are always picking on me because of my clothes and hair. I couldn't take it anymore today, so I just beat one of the girls up pretty bad." James reaches under the seat, grabs his wad of cash, peels off a couple hundred dollar bills, gives them to Teresa, and says, "Lets swing by the mall to get you some clothes." Teresa tries to give the money back to him, but he refuses to take it, so she reluctantly puts the money in her pocket. He gets on the interstate, and heads to the mall. Once at the mall, Teresa buys three outfits and a pair of shoes. She says to James, "My mom is going to want to know where all these clothes came from." James says, "Don't you worry about that. I can handle your momma. You just make sure you don't tell her about me hiding your suspension from her."

After leaving the mall, they stop to grab something to eat at a food truck. On the way home James makes a few stops to sell some weed to a few people. Teresa is terrified that he will get caught by the police while she is with him, so Teresa lies and tells

Chapter 1 – Good Girl Gone Bad?

James that she feels dizzy from getting hit earlier and asks if he can take her home. James agrees and the two head to the house. Once home Teresa runs to her bedroom and attempts to close the door, but James sticks his foot in the doorway to prevent it from closing. A stunned Teresa asks, "What's up?" James responds by saying, "What did your momma say about keeping this door opened?" Teresa says, "Oh I forgot. Well, I'm just going to go sit on the front porch to get some fresh air." As she tries to leave the room, James steps in front of her to prevent her from leaving. Teresa says, "Move please!" James asks, "Do you like your new clothes I gotcha? Do you still want me to keep our little secret? It's time for you to keep your end of the deal." Teresa says, "What are you talking about? What do you want? Here take the clothes back. I don't want them anymore." James says, "You know what I want and it's too late to back out now." Teresa tries to force her way out of the room but James, who is six foot four and weighs two hundred and twenty pounds easily overpowers the much smaller Teresa. James picks Teresa up, throws her on the bed and closes the door.

After about thirty minutes, a sweaty James emerges from the room breathing heavily. He yells for Teresa to get up and take a shower before her mother gets home. Teresa is wrapped in the sheets naked and crying profusely. She finally gets up to take a shower and as she passes James in the hallway he whispers,

Chapter 1 – Good Girl Gone Bad?

"Keep this between me and you or else." After taking a shower, Teresa goes back to her room and cries herself to sleep. James takes a shower and gets dressed. Before leaving, James peaks his head into Teresa's room to check on her and to remind her not to say anything about what just happened. He grabs his gun, money and bag of weed and leaves the house. Teresa falls back to sleep only to be awaken a couple of hours later by her mother telling her to come eat dinner. When Teresa walks into the kitchen her mother and James are already sitting at the table. Fay says, "Girl you were sleeping so peacefully that I didn't want to wake you. You must've had a long day at school." Teresa looks at James and then says, "No, it was the typical school day. I was just up late last night." James says, "Fay I went to the mall today and bought Teresa a few outfits and some shoes. I hope that was ok." "That's fine baby. Teresa can try them on after dinner. Now tell James thank you.", says a smiling Fay. Teresa says, "Thanks Mr. James." Fay reaches over and hugs and kisses James. James winks his eye at Teresa as he hugs Fay. A disgusted Teresa gets up and says, "Mom can I eat dinner in my room? I want to watch television while I eat." Fay says, "Sure baby. Are you ok sweetheart?" Teresa says, "Yes I'm fine mom. Just a little tired." Teresa heads to her bedroom and lays down and immediately falls asleep without touching her dinner. The home phone rings and seeing that it was Teresa's school on the caller ID James

Chapter 1 – Good Girl Gone Bad?

immediately answers it. It's the secretary calling to let Fay know that Teresa had been suspended earlier that day. James tells the secretary that Fay is really busy at the moment and that he would relay the message to her. Teresa is awakened a short time later by her mom telling her to try the clothes on that James bought her. Teresa says to herself, "I know how they fit, I picked them out." Teresa reluctantly gets out of bed, puts on one of the outfits and comes out of her room to model her new clothes for James and Fay. "Damn baby you look good, says Fay. James, you did a good job baby. How did you manage to get the right size? Those clothes fit perfectly." James pauses briefly and says, "Uhh, the girl working at the store was about her size, so I had her try the clothes on. I got lucky I guess." The entire time he was talking, his eyes were fixated on Teresa. "So, do you like the clothes baby?" Fay asks. Teresa forces a smile and says, "I love the clothes mom. Thanks so much Mr. James." Teresa then goes to her room for the rest of the evening.

The following morning a startled Teresa is awakened by James. She screams, "Get out! What do you want?" James covers her mouth and whispers, "You have to get up and pretend you are going to school remember?" Teresa forgot that she didn't tell her mother about her two-day suspension. She jumps up and showers and gets dressed. James gets dressed also, and wakes Fay to tell her that he is going to take Teresa to school since she is

Chapter 1 – Good Girl Gone Bad?

running late and that he will be back later after making some runs. They both leave out of the house and gets into James' car. Teresa asks, "What are we going to do all day?" James looks over at Teresa and smiles and puts his hand on her leg. She slides over closer to the car door, so he can no longer reach her. James laughs and says, "First let's get some breakfast, then we're going to work for a few hours." They go to a small diner and have breakfast. When James gets up to use the restroom the curious waitress notices how uncomfortable Teresa looks and asks her if she is ok. Teresa tells the waitress she is fine and that she has been suspended from school, so her stepdad is watching her while her mom is at work. The waitress asks Teresa how old she is, and when Teresa tells her that she is thirteen, the waitress becomes even more skeptical because Teresa is very small for her age and could pass for a ten or eleven-year-old. Before she could ask any more questions, James comes back to the table and asks the waitress what's going on. The waitress says, "Nothing, just asking the pretty young lady why she isn't in school today." An upset James says, "That's none of your damn business lady, now bring me my check." James pays the tab, and they leave without leaving the waitress a tip. Over the next few hours James meets up with several people selling them small amounts of marijuana. Teresa is so nervous riding with him while he sells drugs that she has to have him pull over so she can vomit. James asks her

Chapter 1 – Good Girl Gone Bad?

what's wrong and Teresa responds by saying, "I'm scared, and I don't want to go to jail like my brother." James says, "Well let's go get some lunch and then I can take you home. Your mom will not be back so you can stay there until she gets off." Teresa doesn't want to be home with James alone again, so she tells him that she needs to meet up with her cousin after school to get her homework assignments. James isn't smart enough to question her as to why she just doesn't just email her homework to her which is what her Pumpkin is actually going to do. Teresa would rather ride around with him while he sells drugs than to be alone with him in that house. After they have lunch, they ride around for a few hours until school lets out. James and Teresa sit in the parking lot of the school until Teresa sees Pumpkin walking down the sidewalk headed home. James pulls up beside her and Teresa yells out the window, "Cuz, slowdown, it's me Teresa" and hops out the car. She gives her a hug and starts to walk with her down the sidewalk. Pumpkin asks, "What are you doing here and who is that man?" Teresa says, "That's my mother's boyfriend James. I had him bring me up here so I can get my homework assignments from you." Pumpkin looks at her puzzled and says, "You know that I'm going to email you your homework assignments. So, tell me why you are really here." "I'm scared to be in the house with him alone again", says Teresa. "Did he do something to you?", Pumpkin asks. Before she can

Chapter 1 – Good Girl Gone Bad?

answer James says, "Come on Teresa, we have to get home now." Teresa whispers to Pumpkin, "I will call you later. Now hand me some papers from your backpack so he will think you are giving me my homework assignments." Pumpkin removes her backpack, unzips it and hands Teresa some old math worksheets and Teresa folds them up and runs back to James' car. James and Teresa then head back home.

Much to Teresa's delight they arrive home just a few minutes before Fay gets there. As Teresa checks her email and begins working on her actual homework and listening to music, the phone rings and it's her cousin Pumpkin. Pumpkin wants to know why she doesn't want to be alone with James anymore. Although she really wants to tell her what happened, Teresa just tells her cousin nothing happened and that she just doesn't like James. After talking for about an hour, the two get off the phone and Teresa finishes up her homework. The following day goes just like the previous one. She rides around with James all day, meets up with Pumpkin after school and then heads home. She is relieved to have made it through another day of being alone with James. This is the last day of her suspension, and she can't wait to attend school the following day. For the remainder of the day, she stays in her room only to come out to eat dinner and shower.

The next morning when she arrives at the bus stop, she expects the kids to start picking with her about the fight and suspension. Much to her surprise, it's the total opposite, they are extremely nice to her. One kid says, "What's up champ?" She is wearing the new shoes James purchased for her and another one of the kids says to her, "Nice shoes Laila Ali." Once she gets to school all of the teachers and other kids welcome her back from her suspension. The kids that normally tease her at school along with the girl she fought all welcome her back and apologize to Teresa for picking on her. Teresa says to herself, "I would've been fought one of them had I known that would make them treat me better." The rest of the school day flies by and before she knows it, school is out and Teresa is on the bus heading home. Her father is waiting in his car in front of the house as she walks home from the bus stop. She can't wait to get away for her weekly visit with her dad, so she runs pass his car and runs in the house and grabs the bag that she already had packed and immediately runs back out to her father's car. Teresa says, "Hi Dad" and gives him a kiss on the cheek and he pulls off. Teresa and Jesse spend the entire weekend watching movies, joking and playing video games. Once Sunday night comes around, Teresa isn't ready to go home, so she tries to come up with reasons to stay longer. First, she tells her father that she doesn't feel good, then she fakes sleep on the couch when Jesse is trying to take her back. During the ride home she says, "Dad turn the car around, we need to go back to your house because I left my phone charger at your place." Jesse says, "No we don't, I have another one for you in the glove box. I've been meaning to give it to you because I was sick of you always saying your phone was dead." Teresa then frantically opens her backpack and says, "I think I left my Science Book at your house. We have to go back and get it. I have a test tomorrow that I need to study for." Jesse responds by saying, "I know you didn't bring your Science Book with you. What's going on with you? Why are you trying to find excuses to stay with me longer?" After thinking about it for a few seconds, Teresa reluctantly says, "Dad can I stay with you instead of with momma?" A shocked Jesse responds to Teresa by saying, "Now as much as I would love for you to stay with me, you know your mother is not having that." Teresa says, "I mean, my school is closer, and I can be closer to Pumpkin." Her dad looks at her and says, "Like I said, now you know your mother is not having that. Why do you want to live with me all of a sudden anyway? Are y'all beefing or something?" Teresa hesitantly says, "Mom has a strange man living there and he really creeps me out." An angry Jesse suddenly starts driving a lot faster. Jesse angrily says, "I'm going to talk to her about that bullshit." When they pull up to the house, he lays on the horn until Fay comes out. Teresa gets out of the car and runs in the house pass her mom without saying a word. Fay comes to the car laughing and says, "What did you do to my baby that got her so upset that she didn't even speak to her own momma?" Jesse angrily responds by saying, "It ain't my fault she's upset. You're the one with some man living here that's making my daughter feel uncomfortable. Fay says, "You don't run nothing over here and neither does she. As a matter of fact, since y'all got so much to say about what goes on over here, you won't be picking up Teresa anymore until I decide it's ok. I will see your black ass in Child Support Court." She storms into the house and busts into Teresa's room and whips Teresa viciously for complaining to her father about James. At this moment Teresa feels that she definitely can't tell her mother about what James did to her.

A month passes and a tired Teresa keeps falling asleep in Math class. The math teacher, Mrs. Henderson, finally gets upset and screams," Teresa what is your problem? You've been late and falling asleep in here every day this week. Please step out and get some water." As Teresa makes it to the door, she stops and vomits in the trash can. This is the second time this week that she has vomited in class. After class, Mrs. Henderson asks Teresa to stay behind so she can have a word with her. Mrs. Henderson says," Teresa I've noticed a lot of change in you and it's not good. Your grades are dropping; your attitude has changed, and you sleep most of the hour away in my class. Let's not forget about the vomiting this week. How are things going at home?" Teresa says," Everything is fine, I just haven't seen my father in a few weeks so I'm a little sad about that. I will be alright Mrs. Henderson." As Teresa starts to walk out, Mrs. Henderson says," Teresa I would like for you to go see the school nurse to take a pregnancy test." An embarrassed and shocked Teresa says," But Mrs. Henderson, I've never..umm, done it." "Well, if that is true then you have absolutely nothing to worry about then, now go", says Mrs. Henderson. She writes a note and hands it to Teresa and tells Teresa to make sure she lets her know the results. Teresa goes to the nurse's office and gives the nurse the note and the nurse tells her to come to the back. After administering the test, the nurse tells Teresa to wait in the lobby. The nurse calls her back ten minutes later and gives her the results and to Teresa's surprise, it's positive. Teresa immediately says, "That can't be correct. Please test me again." The nurse asks Teresa if she knows who the father is. Teresa runs out of the nurse's office crying and spends the rest of her lunch hour sitting in the stairwell. Pumpkin finds Teresa in the stairwell crying and asks her what's been going on with her lately. Hesitantly, Teresa breaks the news to Pumpkin. She says, "I just found out that I am pregnant, and that dirty old man James is the father. He raped me!" Pumpkin hugs Teresa tightly and says, "Lil Cuz you have to tell Aunt Fay what happened to you. You can't let him get away with what he's done to you." Teresa responds by saying, "I can't tell her anything. She will not believe me. She always chooses him over me. Plus, I don't want to start any more trouble at home." After talking to Teresa for a while, Pumpkin finally convinces Teresa that she needs to tell her mother. Teresa assures Pumpkin that she will tell her mother when she gets home from work that evening.

Teresa spends the rest of the day at school, the entire bus ride and walk from the bus stop contemplating how she would break the news to her mother. As she approaches her house, she notices her mother's car is in the driveway. This is strange because her mother usually doesn't make it home before her. She walks in and sees that her mother is sitting in the living room with all the lights turned out. Teresa says," Ma, I have something I really need to tell you." Fay looks up with tears in her eyes and says," Well I have something to tell you also. Sit down sweetheart." Teresa takes a seat on the couch next to her mother. Fay grabs both of Teresa's hands and says," Baby I am sorry, but your father passed away today. He was involved in a bad car accident this afternoon." Teresa and Fay both begin to cry uncontrollably. Fay consoles Teresa for about thirty minutes and then she finally asks Teresa what it was that she needed to tell her. Thinking at that moment wasn't the appropriate time to say anything about her pregnancy, she tells her mother it wasn't important and that it was just some schoolgirl gossip. Teresa and Fay cry until they both fall asleep on the couch. Teresa is awakened by James busting into the house and yelling at Fay. James screams, "Why in the hell are you crying over that damn fool? He left your monkey ass high and dry." Fay screams," To hell with you!" James immediately punches Fay in the face and tells her to watch her damn mouth. Teresa jumps up off the couch and screams, "Don't you hit my momma again and don't say nothing else about my daddy either." James just smirks and walks towards the front door. Fay says, "James please don't go, and Teresa mind your damn business. This ain't got nothing to do with you." Teresa runs back into her room and slams the door and that's where she remains for the remainder of the night. With Fay pleading with him to stay, James still leaves the house that night and vows to never come back. However, with nowhere to really go, he returns three days later and the following week Teresa, Fay and James all attend Jesse's funeral.

A week after the funeral, Teresa finally returns to school. Her father's death, James still living at her house and her being pregnant with his child are all taking their toll on Teresa and her behavior begins to change drastically. She sleeps in class most of the time and when she is awake, she constantly disrupts the class by talking and starting fights with the other kids. After a week of behaving like this, she is finally suspended. This time the principal immediately calls her mother and tells her that Teresa has been suspended from school again. Once Fay gets home, she goes into Teresa's room and has a talk with Teresa about her behavior. She understands that it's probably due to her father's death, so she isn't that hard on her. She just tells her she must find a better way to deal with her father's death. As Fay is walking out of Teresa's room it occurs to her that the principal said that Teresa had been suspended again. Fay says, "Hold up, is this your second time being suspended from school? The principal said that you have been suspended again. Last time I checked, again means that something has happened before." James immediately jumps off the couch when he hears Fay's question. Teresa says, "Yes ma'am, I'm sorry. I got into a fight and was suspended a few weeks ago." Just as Fay takes the belt from around her waist, James runs into the room gets in front of her to prevent her from getting to Teresa. The always manipulative James sees this as another opportunity to earn Teresa's trust and loyalty. James says, "It's all my fault baby. I was just trying to win her over so she could accept me staying here. I told her not to tell you about the suspension and I helped her cover it up. I didn't tell you that the school called here to tell you that she had been suspended. I'm so sorry baby." A visibly upset Fay accepts his apology and tells the both of them that this better not happen again. Teresa wants to tell her mother exactly what happened that day badly, but she knows it would break her mother's heart if she told her.

Chapter 1 – Good Girl Gone Bad?

The following day after Fay leaves for work, James comes into Teresa's room while she is laying down and sits on her bed and puts his hand on her leg. She pushes his hand away and sits up on the bed. James says, "Come on now baby, you owe me after I saved your ass yesterday." Teresa screams, "I am pregnant by you, asshole!" James jumps up off of the bed and asks her how she knows that it's his. Teresa says, "It's definitely yours. I had never done it until you did what you did to me." James says, "You can't tell your mother about this. I'm already on parole and I'm not about to go back to prison over this. You're getting an abortion and we are going to act like none of this ever happened. Just give me a couple of days to get the money together and we can get it done. OK?" Once Teresa agrees that she will have an abortion James heads out. Teresa spends most of the day doing homework, listening to music and on the internet. She is relieved that she will be soon resolving her pregnancy issue. After her mother makes it home from work the phone rings. Teresa answers the phone and there is an automated voice on the other end saying, "You have a collect call from a correctional facility. To accept the call please press five." Teresa is excited because she thinks she will get to hear from her older brother but is shocked to hear James' voice after she accepts the call. James was caught with a small amount of marijuana and a gun after leaving the house earlier that day. Teresa says,

Chapter 1 – Good Girl Gone Bad?

"Hello, what are you doing in jail? How are you going to pay for the.." Before Teresa can finish her sentence, James cuts her off and says to Teresa, "Shut up and put your momma on the phone." When Teresa gives the phone to Fay, James tells Fay that he needs five thousand dollars to get out of jail. However, Fay doesn't have any money since she spent her last on Jesse's funeral and she is barely making it without the money Jesse was giving her weekly to help out. James is so upset that he hangs up the phone on Fay. If James doesn't get the money, he will have to remain in jail until his court date, which is in six months. A panicking Teresa says to her mother, "What's going on momma?" To which Fay replies, "It's none of your damn business what's going on, just know that James will not be around here for a few months." Teresa is visibly upset so Fay says, "What the hell are you mad for? I know you are glad that he's gone." Teresa thinks that now may be the perfect time to tell her mom the truth about what James did to her. Teresa says, "Ma, I have something to tell you. James forced himself on me and now I'm pregnant with his child. Please don't be mad at me I'm so sorry." Expecting sympathy from Fay, Teresa starts crying and attempts to hug her mother, but Fay pushes her away and slaps her. Fay starts crying and accuses Teresa of lying on James. Teresa pleads with her mother to believe her, but Fay says, "So your little fast ass goes out here and gets pregnant and you want to blame it on my man so you can get him locked up? Is that right? Call your grandmother because you can't stay here anymore." Teresa calls her grandmother to let her know what's going on and packs up her belongings. Fay drives Teresa over to her grandmother's home and helps her remove her belongings from the car and drives off. Teresa walks in the house and is greeted with a hug from her grandmother and her cousin Pumpkin.

The next couple of months are really hard for Teresa. She is still living with her grandmother; James is still in jail and by the time her mother saves enough money to pay for the abortion she is too far along to have the procedure done. So, she will be having a child at thirteen. She considered adoption but she's somewhat become enamored with the idea of being a mother now. The further along Teresa gets the less interested she is in school. She gets a part time job at a small market as a cashier and uses the money to buy items to prepare for the arrival of her baby. The owner is friends with her grandmother, so she allows Teresa to work although she is under aged and pays her in cash. She goes from being a straight A student to failing most of her classes in a couple of months. She doesn't listen to anything her grandmother says and her resentment towards her mother and James grows more and more every day. She hardly even listens to Pumpkin anymore. She misses more and more days from school due to having doctors' appointments and being ill and eventually she just stops attending school altogether. After missing a couple of weeks of school, her grandmother finally talks her into going back and finishing the school year, which she eventually does, and she passes to the eighth grade.

In the beginning of the summer, a day after her fourteenth birthday, Teresa goes into labor. While in the delivery room with Pumpkin and her grandmother there is a commotion in the hallway. A woman can be heard saying," That's my baby in there. Let me in." A few seconds later Fay busts in the delivery room and says, "I hope you didn't think I wasn't going to show up to see the birth of my first grandchild." Although Teresa is in pain, she is able to smile and tell her mom that she loves her. After several hours of labor, Teresa gives birth to a baby boy, that she names after her father Jesse. Once Teresa is released from the hospital, she moves back in with her mother. Things go fine for the first summer with Teresa watching Jesse during the day while Fay works and Fay watching him in the evenings while Teresa works. They never mention James at all. Once school starts, Fay changes her schedule at the salon to second shift so she can watch Jesse during the day. Teresa is back to making good grades in school and is currently only working on the weekends at the store. Everyone is helping Teresa out including Pumpkin who watches Jesse on Friday nights for her. A couple of years go by,

Chapter 1 – Good Girl Gone Bad?

and Teresa has even found a boyfriend, a seventeen-year-old kid from school named Eric. They have been dating for about one month. Things are going great but all of that would be changed by a knock on the door. Expecting her boyfriend, Teresa with Jesse in her arms opens the door and much to her surprise the person at the door is James. Not only is she shocked that he had enough nerve to come there, but she is also shocked because he was originally sentenced to ten years in prison. James says, "Aren't you going to let me in?" Teresa refuses to let him in the house and immediately calls her mother. After a heated argument with Fay, Teresa reluctantly opens the door for James. Teresa finds out that Fay has been keeping in touch with James the entire time he was incarcerated and has decided to let him come stay at the house again. James walks in with his bags in hand and takes a seat on the couch. He asks if he can hold Jesse and Teresa just ignores him and goes to her room and closes her door. Teresa is extremely nervous with James in the house. She is relieved once Eric finally shows up, followed shortly by the arrival of her mother Fay. As soon as her mother arrives Teresa runs out her room and says, "Why is he here momma?" Fay responds by saying, "This is my damn house girl and whoever I want to stay here can stay here. If you don't like that you can get the hell out again. I'm sure your grandma will welcome you back." Eric comes out of Teresa's room and says, "No disrespect

Chapter 1 – Good Girl Gone Bad?

Ms. Fay, but if Teresa don't like this dude, then he shouldn't be here. But anyway, Teresa can come crash at my crib. My mom won't mind." Eric stays in an apartment with his mother and older cousin. He says they have an extra room that she can use. Teresa is reluctant at first thinking she could just go to her grandmother's instead until Fay says to Eric, "Boy get your narrow ass out of my house and take my disrespectful child with you." Teresa immediately goes into her room and gathers some of her belongings and load them into Eric's car and they leave and head to Eric's apartment.

Once at Eric's house, he gives Teresa a few house rules that she must follow if she is going to stay there. Eric tells Teresa that when his cousin is home that she needs to stay in the bedroom and not to come out unless it's an emergency and under no circumstance is she to answer the door and do not bother his mom when her door is closed. Teresa finds the rules odd, but she agrees to stay anyway. Eric's mom, Tina comes out of her room to finally meet Teresa. With her speech slurred Tina says, "Hey baby. Glad to finally meet you. I've heard so much about you. Child go ahead make yourself at home." She tells Teresa that she can watch Jesse during the day while she and Eric are at school. Eric quickly reminds his mom that he's not going to school in the morning. The following morning, Teresa gets ready for school and on her way out she sees Eric and two other men are in the living room. One of the men is Eric's cousin Malik. The other man hands some money to Malik and leaves the apartment. Eric introduces Teresa to Malik and tells Teresa he will take Jesse into the room with his mom once he wakes up. Teresa asks Eric why he isn't going to school, and he says he has to help Malik do some work around the apartment. Once Teresa arrives at school, she finds Pumpkin and tells her what happened and that she now lives with Eric and his mother. Pumpkin shows her disapproval and says she is going to ask their grandma if Teresa can move back in. Teresa declines the offer and says she will be fine living with Eric and his mother. Pumpkin knows that Teresa will no longer be welcome in her grandmother's home once she hears about this, so she continues to plead with Teresa to tell their grandma she needed a place to stay. Unfortunately, her pleas fall on deaf ears.

Teresa's first couple of weeks staying with Eric go smoothly. The only odd things she notices are that Eric's mom rarely leaves her room and that his cousin Malik tends to show up every morning as she is leaving for school but is gone when she gets home. One night while Jesse is asleep in the room with Eric's mom, Eric comes into the room with Teresa and gets in the bed with her. She immediately jumps out the bed. Since she has been staying there, Eric has been sleeping on the couch. Eric says, "What's wrong? It's about time we did this." Teresa tells

Chapter 1 – Good Girl Gone Bad?

Eric she's not ready and he responds by asking," When will you be ready then?" She says to Eric, "Well, I have never actually done it." "Wait, what?" Eric replies. You do know you have a whole baby that you gave birth to in the next room?" Teresa sits up and says, "I have something to tell you. James raped me and got me pregnant. I told my mom and she didn't believe me." When she first met Eric, she told him that the child's father moved away with his parents without knowing that she was pregnant. Eric jumps up and screams, "I am going to kill that motherfucker. I swear to god!" Teresa is shocked because she has never seen Eric act like this. She gets up and hugs Eric and tells him not to do anything and that everything is ok now. She then begins kissing Eric and leads him to the bed.

The following morning Teresa wakes up and Eric is no longer in the bed with her. She looks at the clock and sees that it is 9 am already so she is already late for school and decides that she just isn't going to go. She jumps out of bed to check on Jesse, but Eric's mom's door is shut. Although she remembers that Eric told her to never disturb his mom, she knocks on the door anyway because she really wants to see Jesse. Eric hears the knocking and screams, "Bitch didn't I tell you to never disturb my mom. What the hell is wrong with you?" Teresa comes running to the front room and says, "Who do you think you are talking to?" Eric immediately slaps Teresa, and Teresa falls to the floor. As she is getting up, she notices both Malik and Eric have guns in their waistbands and there is another man in the house and a large amount of marijuana is on the table. At this moment she realizes that Eric and his cousin deal drugs out of the apartment during the day. That explains how Eric can give her money to help with Jesse, have a car and the nice clothes he wears. It also explains why he is always missing school. He initially told Teresa the money he has is the money from the life insurance company after his father passed, which she will soon find out is a lie. His father is alive and well. Eric just hasn't seen him in years. Before Teresa can say anything, Tina stumbles out of her room with Jesse and begins screaming incoherently at Eric. She mumbles, "Boy don't you hit that girl no more. What's wrong with you? That's what your monkey ass daddy locked up for." She is obviously high and Teresa notices that she still has a needle hanging from her arm. Teresa runs and grabs Jesse and goes into her room and shuts and locks the door. Once Eric and Malik wrap up their drug transaction Eric goes into the back and busts into Teresa's room. Teresa and Jesse are dressed, and she is packing her bags. Eric says," Where do you think you are going?" Teresa doesn't answer and just continues to pack up her belongings. Then Teresa says, "You never told me you were a drug dealer and that your mom was on drugs. I've been leaving Jesse with her all day in a damn trap house. Not to mention that

Chapter 1 – Good Girl Gone Bad?

you just hit me. I have to get the hell out of here." Eric apologizes for everything and begs her to stay. He promises to never hit her again, but unfortunately, that was just the first of the many times that his fist would find its way to her face. Teresa is stuck between a rock and a hard place. James is still staying with her mother and her grandmother has cut her off, so Teresa feels she has no choice but to stay with Eric and his mother.

A year goes by and the abuse from Eric only gets worse. She is missing school more and more because she doesn't want everyone to see the bruises that remain after Eric's numerous beatings. The abuse only stops once Teresa discovers that she is once again pregnant. Teresa is now seventeen years old with a three-year-old son and pregnant with another child. She wants to move out, but she can't save any money because Eric takes the little money that she makes from working her job at the store. She eventually gives birth to another son who she names Eric after his father. A few years pass and things are extremely rough for Teresa and her kids. Her job at the store and the fact that her kids are doing extremely well in school are the only two things that she can smile about. Eric is constantly in and out of jail and he's now doing drugs, so the apartment is filled with his addict friends daily and his abusive ways only get worse. He beats her so badly that she spends a couple of weeks in the hospital. This beating also leads to Eric getting incarcerated and being sentenced to a year in jail, which is the longest that he has ever been sentenced to do. After being released from the hospital Teresa comes home to an apartment full of strangers. With Eric in jail, Tina has turned the apartment into a full fledge drug den. Teresa immediately runs to the back to find Jesse and Eric. She busts in Tina's room and yells," Where the hell are my kids?" Tina is so high that she can't speak. She just points in the direction of Teresa's room. She goes to the room and finds the door is locked so she starts banging on the door. She then hears Jesse say, "Go away." Teresa says, "It's me baby. Open the door." Jesse opens the door and Teresa screams, "Where is your brother?" Jesse points to the bed and says," I didn't want the bad people to hurt him." Jesse has built a makeshift fort using pillows to attempt to hide Eric. Teresa hugs both Eric and Jesse and begins to cry. She tells them both that she will get them out of this situation.

The following morning, she calls her mother and tells her the predicament she has found herself in. Teresa and Fay have been talking off and on over the last couple of years and Teresa has found herself going back to live with her mom after many of the beatings she received from Eric. Eric would always apologize and talk her into coming back, so after her last visit, Fay told Teresa that if she goes back with Eric not to come back to her looking for a place to stay. Fay stands by what she told Teresa

Chapter 1 – Good Girl Gone Bad?

and tells her she cannot stay at her house. Teresa pleads with Fay, but Fay doesn't budge. Teresa has nowhere to go since her grandmother has passed and Pumpkin has returned from college but is living with her boyfriend. She needs to find a place to stay so she is forced to pick up more hours at the store. She works seven days a week at twelve hours a day while occasionally taking money from the register. Eric and Jesse come to the store most days after school and stays there until she gets off. Each day she comes home to a house full of drug users, dealers and other seedy individuals. Although she keeps her door locked, some days she actually has to kick people out of her bedroom or fight because someone has stolen some of her belongings. Teresa, Jesse and Eric spend most nights locked in her bedroom scared.

After a few months of saving, Teresa can finally afford to rent a small two-bedroom apartment along with purchasing some decent used furniture. Although her new place is in a rougher part of town, she feels that anything is better than her previous living arrangement. A few years pass and everything is going fine although she can barely afford her place, so she is still stealing money from work to make ends meet. Teresa enrolls in classes to get her GED and her and Fay are on better terms now. One night while at her apartment there is a knock on the door. Teresa, who isn't expecting anyone makes her way to the door and is shocked when she looks through the peephole. The voice

Chapter 1 – Good Girl Gone Bad?

on the other side of the door says, "It's me. I know you are in there, so open up." Teresa finally opens the door and Eric is standing there smiling holding some flowers and a duffle bag. Teresa says, "What are you doing here?" A surprised Eric says, "What's wrong? I thought you would be happy to see me." Teresa responds by saying, "I am, I just didn't know you were out." She gives him a hug and lets him in. Teresa and Eric have been talking off and on over the last couple of months and he has come to stay with her and the kids in between his numerous stints in jail. Eric says, "Everything will be different this time, I promise." He walks over and gives Teresa a kiss. Going against her better judgement, Teresa allows Eric to stay. This would be one of many times that she allows him back. Eric eventually gets his act together and the family is doing fine but all of that would change with one event. One Saturday as Teresa is attempting to leave the store, she discovers that the front door has been locked. She notifies her boss, and she responds by saying, "I know, I'm the one who locked it." A confused Teresa says, "I need to get home. Can you unlock the door for me ma'am?" There is a knock on the door and the storeowner makes her way pass Teresa and opens the door. It's the police. The owner says to Teresa, "While doing the books, we realized we were short a few thousand dollars. We looked at the surveillance video and saw you taking money on several occasions. Why did you do this?

Chapter 1 – Good Girl Gone Bad?

Haven't we been good to you?" Teresa doesn't answer, she just turns around and puts her hands behind her back and says, "Can you call my mom and my boyfriend to tell them what's going on?" Her boss agrees to do so.

This is Teresa's first time going to jail so she is terrified. After spending two days in a holding cell, she is finally allowed to make a phone call. The first person she calls is Eric. She calls several times, and he doesn't answer. She then calls her mother. When Fay answers Teresa immediately says, "How are the kids?" Much to Teresa's surprise Fay responds by saying, "I don't know, I guess they are with their Daddy." Teresa screams, "What the hell do you mean you don't know. Why aren't they with you? I can't get a hold of Eric." "When the store called and told me what happened I called him too and got no answer. I'm going through some shit right now Teresa and I can't be watching no damn kids", says Fay. Teresa screams, "What's more important than your grandkids? Well can you at least help me bond out?" Fay says, "Baby I'm not doing too well. I was diagnosed with heart disease a year ago and the doctors are saying that I'm not going to make it much longer. I'm not able to do a lot for myself right now let alone for the kids. I haven't been able to work much, and all of my money has been spent on my medical bills. I can't even afford to keep this house. I'm so sorry baby. I wanted to tell you a while ago." Teresa begins crying and says, "What

Chapter 1 – Good Girl Gone Bad?

about James? Why isn't he helping you out?" Fay says, "I haven't seen that piece of shit James in over six months. When he was around, he wasn't helping me anyway. I think he was just sticking around hoping to get the house if I passed away." Teresa says, "Mom I'm so sorry. I will find a way out of here to help you out. I promise. I love you." Unbeknownst to Teresa this would be the last time she would get to speak to her mother. She passes away a week later while Teresa is still in the county jail. The county jail does allow Teresa to get out to view her mother's body, but she is immediately returned to jail afterwards.

Teresa calls Eric several times a day everyday for a week straight and all of her calls go unanswered. She leaves so many messages that his mailbox is eventually full. She even calls the store where she once worked and when the owner heard it was Teresa, she didn't accept the call. Teresa was only calling to see if she could possibly check on her kids for her, but the storeowner assumed that she was calling to try to convince her to drop the charges against her. She decides to try to call Eric one more time and he finally answers this time. Teresa screams, "Where the hell have you been? Where are my damn kids?" In a slurred voice, Eric says, "The kids are just fine. I've been working extra hours to pay your bond." In reality, he has been doing the total opposite. He's lost his job and has even lost the bill money by trying to flip it on some drugs. He's back on drugs and hasn't been home since

Chapter 1 – Good Girl Gone Bad?

a couple of days after she went to jail, yet he tells her that everything is fine. The rent, electric amongst other bills were past due the day she went to jail, so she asks Eric if he's paid any of them. Once again, he lies and tells her that all the bills were paid and tells her not to worry. Teresa believes his lies and tells him that she will call back tomorrow. However, when she calls back the following day, Eric's phone has been turned off. She is frantic. She calls him daily over the next couple of weeks until she gives up and decides to call her cousin Pumpkin. She and Pumpkin have kept in touch over the years, and she has occasionally borrowed money from her. Pumpkin agrees to pay her bond and comes down to pick Teresa up. Teresa comes out and immediately gives Pumpkin a hug and says, "Thanks cuz, I promise I will pay you every cent back. That was the longest month of my life." Pumpkin says, "No need to pay me back. Hold up, what do you mean one month? Where are the kids and why are you just now asking me for money?" Although she has no idea about what's been going on with the kids, she tells Pumpkin that Eric has been taking care of them and they are doing great. Pumpkin gives Teresa a ride home and tells her to call her if she needs anything. Teresa tells Pumpkin that she loves her and gets out the car and runs to her apartment looking for the kids.

Chapter 1 – Good Girl Gone Bad?

Once Teresa makes it to her apartment, she takes an eviction notice off of the front door, unlocks the door and goes inside. She puts the notice on the coffee table and begins searching the apartment for Eric. She attempts to turn on the lights and finds that the power has been turned off. She must make some money fast. She washes up and leaves the apartment in search of Eric. She stops at a pay phone, calls Eric, and discovers that his number is still disconnected. She stops by all of his normal hangouts, but he is nowhere to be found. Knowing that she will need money fast she eventually catches a bus to the mall to fill out job applications. She visits almost every store in the mall to apply for jobs and finds that most of the stores aren't hiring. As a frustrated Teresa makes her way to the mall's exit, she hears a familiar voice say, "Baby girl, where you headed in such a hurry". She turns around and much to her surprise, James is standing behind her. He notices tears in her eyes and he asks her what's going on. Teresa hesitantly tells James everything that's been going on with her, including the fact that she just got out of jail and that she is about to be evicted. James says to Teresa, "If you need some cash fast, I can help you with that. My homeboy is having a bachelor party at his crib tonight and I'm in charge of the entertainment." Teresa cuts him off and says, "Excuse you, I'm not a damn stripper." James laughs and says, "I wasn't talking about you stripping, you can just serve drinks.

Chapter 1 – Good Girl Gone Bad?

Look, I can get you a little skirt and some heels and you can probably make one thousand dollars on tips tonight, on top of the five hundred dollars I'm going to pay you." Teresa says, "Just serving drinks and nothing else? I can do that. I really need the money. Thank you." They turn around and go to a few stores and James purchases an outfit for Teresa to wear later that night. Once they are done shopping, James gives Teresa a ride home so she can take a shower and get dressed. James waits in the car while Teresa goes inside. Teresa comes in to find that Jesse and Eric still haven't made it home. She takes a shower and puts on her new outfit and heads out to James' car. She gets in and says to James, "My kids still aren't home. Let's wait around a little longer or at least let me run back in to leave them a note." James responds by saying, "Look, you haven't seen them in a month so what's one more night. If you leave a note, they are going to be waiting on you to get home. This party will last all night. You can surprise them in the morning. Plus, we are already late. Now let's go get this money." She agrees and they head to the party.

They drive for about thirty minutes until they pull up to a nice home in a beautiful subdivision. Teresa looks nervous so James tells her to relax and pulls a pill from his pocket and tells her to take it. Teresa is hesitant at first, but James convinces her that the pill will help her relax. The pill immediately kicks in and

Chapter 1 – Good Girl Gone Bad?

Teresa and James head into the party. There are guys and strippers all over the house. A few hours pass and Teresa is enjoying herself and the money that she is making. In a few hours, she has already made enough money to pay the rent for a couple of months. She doesn't normally drink but she is taking shots of tequila and on top of that she has taken another pill. She even gets a lap dance from one of the girls and gives a lap dance to the bachelor, Lil Rod. That lap dance she gives to Lil Rod would end up being a fatal mistake. At about 7 am Lil Rod pulls James to the side and tells him that he is really feeling Teresa. James laughs and says, "All these women in here that will get with you, and you want to get with the waitress." Lil Rod replies, "She is going to get with me too and you're going to make it happen." He gives James a stack of cash and tells him to ask her to come on to the bedroom." James can't tell him no. He's a major drug dealer from the neighborhood and James wants to be a part of his organization so he takes the money and goes to get Teresa. James approaches Teresa and whispers to her that Lil Rod wants to see her in the back. Teresa who is now extremely drunk says, "What does he want with lil old me?" James lies and says, "I don't know, he probably just wants another lap dance." James shakes his head as Teresa heads to the back because he knows what Lil Rod wants. Teresa knocks on the door and then walks into the room. Lil Rod is laying in the bed with his shirt off.

Chapter 1 – Good Girl Gone Bad?

Teresa says, "James said you wanted to see me. What's up?" He responds by saying, "You know what's up. Now get over here." "So, you want another lap dance?", asks a now nervous Teresa. Lil Rod says, "I want a little more than that baby girl. Now get over here." Teresa although still intoxicated understands exactly what he wants and says, "You're cute and all but I can't do that. I'm just here to serve drinks. Maybe one of the other girls can help you out." He jumps off the bed and screams, "I know what you were here for, but you just got a promotion. Plus, I already paid James for this." Teresa yells, "You paid James for what? I ain't no damn prostitute." Hearing the commotion James comes into the room to see what's going on. Teresa asks, "Did you promise this asshole that I would sleep with him for money?" James just drops his head and doesn't say anything. Teresa says, "James take me home." As Teresa heads towards the door Lil Rod says, "Aren't you forgetting something?" Teresa turns around with a puzzled look on her face. Rod approaches her and takes the apron from around her waist that contains all of her tips and the money James paid her. Teresa screams, "You can't do that. Please, I'm sorry. I really need that money." Lil Rod says," Get the hell out. And you will need to find another way home because me and James have some business to take care of. Now disappear." James grabs Teresa by the arm, drags her to the front door, and pushes her out. Now Teresa, who is drunk and high with no money in an unfamiliar neighborhood, must find her way home. As she staggers through the subdivision, she catches the attention of several of the men due to her wearing a short skirt and heels. After walking a few blocks, she sees Terry walking his dog. He is the first black guy she's seen out in the neighborhood, so she feels like he will be more likely to help her out. However, after being propositioned by Lil Rod and in her drunken and high state of mind, instead of asking for a ride or money she says to Terry, "Are you looking for a good time?" As Terry walks away waiving to a neighbor, Mr. Charles, Teresa tries to understand why she would say such a thing. As she sits on the curb holding the fifty dollars Terry gave her a car pulls up slowly. The older model car contains an older white man. He asks her if she needs any help and Teresa who has halfway nodded off tells the man she needs a ride and has fifty dollars to pay him. The gentleman gets out of the car and as he looks around, helps Teresa into the passenger seat of his car. After Teresa gives him the address, she immediately falls asleep. After about thirty minutes Teresa is awakened with the man on top of her attempting to remove her underwear. They struggle for several minutes as Teresa screams for help at the top of her lungs, but her pleas go unanswered.

Chapter 2
Shorty Wanna Be A Thug?

Chapter 2 – Shorty Wanna Be A Thug?

After returning from walking Mimi, Terry goes into the bedroom and tells Stacey about the encounter he just had with the young woman on the street. Terry puts Mimi in her cage, showers, gets dressed and leaves for work. He rides by the spot where he last saw Teresa. He feels bad about how he had talked to her earlier and was going to offer her a ride, but now she is nowhere to be found. Terry arrives at DelMar Technologies, where he is employed as the Director of Hardware Implementations. As soon as he walks in, he is greeted with a cup of coffee from his assistant and a list of issues that his team is dealing with. He checks a few emails and calls an emergency meeting to discuss the issues for the day. His team recently performed a major server and desktop refresh for a very large pharmaceutical company and things aren't going as planned. His technician that was supposed to be onsite didn't show up, users can't log in to computers and some of the servers aren't setup properly. After an hour-long meeting in which Terry and his team construct a plan of attack, he heads over to the customer's location for a meeting with their C Level employees to smooth things over. On his way he stops and gets a box of doughnuts and some coffee for the meeting. The meeting lasts for about 2 hours, most of which is spent with Terry apologizing for the issues and downtime that was caused by his team's mistakes.

Chapter 2 – Shorty Wanna Be A Thug?

After the meeting Terry is so frustrated that he considers just leaving for the day and going to a bar. Instead, he decides to go grab a bite to eat at his favorite restaurant, a fish and chicken spot named Troy's in his old neighborhood. When he walks in, he walks past a teenager carrying a bag of food and he wonders why the kid isn't in school. He makes his way to the counter and is greeted by the owner, Troy, saying, "What's up T Money, long time no see. I thought you forgot about us poor folks down here in the hood." Terry laughs and says, "Get out of here man, it's only been a couple of months since I've been down here to visit. Anyway, man let me get a fish sandwich with fries and a large Coke." Sensing Terry's frustration, Troy says, "So you had a long half day at work?" Terry laughs and as he looks around, he notices that the lunch crowd is much smaller than it was in the past. He asks Troy how's business to which Troy replies, "Take a look around. We are struggling big time man. I just had to let one of my best workers go today. We need an influx of cash so we can do some more marketing or something. Now I know you can help us with that big money." As Terry gets his food he says to Troy," Yeah, we can talk about that, but first you need to get rid of these knuckleheads hanging out front. They're probably running all the customers away." Troy says," alright bet and don't forget that you were one of those knuckleheads hanging out front not too long ago yourself." Terry smirks, nods his head in agreement, and walks out of the restaurant.

As he steps outside, stops, and looks around briefly, he hears a voice coming from the side of the building. He turns and sees that it's the young man that he walked past as he was entering the restaurant. The young man says to Terry, "Are you straight? What you looking for?" Terry says to the young man, "What do you mean what am I looking for?" The young man says, "I got coke, X, heroin, you name it I got it." Terry responds by saying, "Do I look like a damn junkie? Come to someone else with that bullshit." The young man says, "Well if you not trying to buy nothing then you need to step off Carlton Banks." As they go back and forth a man comes from the side of the building and says, "My apologies Terry, it's the young man's first day on the job, he doesn't know any better." Terry laughs and says, "Man what up Trey?" They shake hands and hug as Terry says, "Teach this young man some damn manners." Trey then says to the young man," JR, this is my homeboy T Money. We go way back. Now apologize to the man." Terry says, "It's all good Trey. Now that I think about it, we were approaching any and everybody that walked down this block also. Hell, that's how I got busted for the first and last time. But look, I have to roll man. Good seeing you Trey, and JR take your lil bad ass to school. This ain't

Chapter 2 – Shorty Wanna Be A Thug?

what's up lil homie." A scared JR shakes his head and mumbles to himself, "Mane I know, but if you only knew."

Five years earlier, a nine-year-old JR walks in on his father beating his mother. This has been a constant thing for as long as JR can remember, and he has had enough. JR says, "Daddy please stop hitting my momma. I'm sick of this. I'm going to mess you up if you don't stop." His father, Big E, turns and says, "Lil boy, What you gonna do? And I ain't your damn daddy so stop calling me that." JR is aware that Big E isn't his real father, but he calls him dad since he's been with his mom most of his life. Big E is actually just his younger brother's father. JR's eyes fill with tears as he drops his head. Big E laughs and says, "I was almost proud of you for a minute. You showed a little heart now you're back to being your old soft self. Mane go get your backpack so you can head to school before you're next." His mom, Tee Tee, as people in the neighborhood call her, looks at JR and nods her head so he reluctantly goes to his room and gets his backpack and his basketball and he and his younger brother head to school. As he walks out of the door of his apartment with his little brother following, he can hear Big E continuing to beat his mother. He thinks about going back in, but he just continues walking down the hall.

His apartment is in a pretty rough part of town and getting out of the building is a daily adventure. He first has to step over Willie the Whino, who always falls asleep in the hallway most nights because he's too drunk to make it into his apartment. Willie always wakes up and gives JR some drunken words of advice. On this particular morning he wakes up and says, "Son, things will get better. Just be strong." He then takes a swig from his bottle and goes back to sleep. Willie and JR talk a lot and he is somewhat JR's best friend. JR loves basketball and Willie was a High School Basketball All American in his younger years and he never misses an opportunity to talk about it. As usual, the elevator is out of order, so JR and his brother have to make their way down sixteen flights of stairs to get to the lobby. Once outside the building, JR makes his way up the street and sees the neighborhood drug dealers all gathered around in front of Troy's Chicken and Fish. They are all decked out in expensive clothing and expensive jewelry while loud music blares from their expensive cars. One of the drug dealers says, "What's up JR, you ready to get some of this fast cash like your boy Lil Randy here?" JR says no thank you, I'm good Trey. Another man can be heard saying, "Leave the lil man alone, as much as he has that ball with him, he's gonna be getting that NBA money one day." JR continues to dribble the ball and walks up the street. Lil Randy runs over and begins to walk with JR and his lil brother, Lil E. "Yo, what's up JR", says an out of breath Randy. "Why you be dissing Trey like that?" JR just shrugs his shoulders, and doesn't answer, but instead asks Randy if he's coming to school today. Before Randy can answer Trey yells out, "Hey Randy leave the square alone and get your ass back down here. We got customers." As Randy runs off, he says to JR, "Forget going to school, come work for Trey with me. It's easy money. Plus, you can make enough to replace those bum ass Pro Wings you're wearing. Come by when school is out." Randy is one of JR's best friends and classmates although he rarely comes to school. He spends most days selling drugs and being a lookout for Trey's crew. He and JR hang out playing video games and shooting ball whenever he isn't working.

As JR and Lil E approach the front door of the school, JR remembers that he's brought his basketball with him, so he empties his backpack and puts the ball in it. JR always grabs his basketball whenever he is nervous or stressed about his home life. He's accidentally brought the ball to school on several other occasions. After putting the ball in his backpack, he ties his little brother's shoes and tells him to meet him in front of the building as soon as school lets out. He gives Lil E a fist bump and then they both head into the school. Once JR walks into his class his teacher, Mrs. Johnson, notices that his backpack looks full, but he has an arm full of books and folders. She calls for JR to come to her desk and tells him to open the backpack and give her the basketball. As he hands her the ball she says, "You had another rough morning." He just drops his head as she tells him he will get the ball back at the end of the day.

As soon as JR makes his way to his seat, someone hits him with a piece of paper. He turns and says, "Today ain't the day for all that playing so stop." The other kids giggle as another piece of paper hits JR. Mrs. Johnson begins the day's lesson with math. As she begins some of the kids continue to laugh and play. JR turns and says," Ssshhh, I can't hear." One of the kids says, "Shut your dusty ass up. You know all of this stuff anyway." JR turns back around and continues to listen to Mrs. Johnson. Mrs. Johnson says, "So who in the class knows what five times seven is?" JR quickly raises his hand and says, "thirty-five." The kid next to JR throws another piece of paper at him and screams, "Nerd!" JR immediately jumps out of his seat and he and the kid begin to fight. Mrs. Johnson runs over and grabs JR and the other kid by the back of their shirts and escorts them to the principal's office. Once in the office, the guidance counselor Mrs. Smith, comes in and begins to talk with JR. She says, "So JR, what's your problem today?" As he begins to tell her about the kids picking on him and throwing paper, she cuts him off and says, "I'm asking about the problems at home." JR drops his head and doesn't say anything. She asks again and this time JR responds by saying, "Look, I am tired and hungry and just want to go back to class." JR quickly apologizes for his outburst and asks Mrs.

Chapter 2 – Shorty Wanna Be A Thug?

Smith if he can please go back to class. She hands him an apple off of the principal's desk and tells him he can leave after he eats the apple. Before leaving she tells him to come see her whenever he is ready to talk. After finishing the apple, he heads back to the classroom. Once he enters the classroom Mrs. Johnson asks, "Are you ready to behave JR?" As JR takes a seat he says, "Yes Ma'am." She then tells JR to open his Spelling book to page one hundred and twenty. For the remainder of the day JR daydreams about basketball and only thinks about hooking up with Lil' Randy when school is out. He's made up his mind that he's going to work for Trey to get enough money to get some decent clothes and so he, Lil E and his mother can all move away from Big E.

Once the bell rings to dismiss school, JR runs to the front to get his basketball and heads out front to meet Lil E. When he gets to the front of the school, he notices that his little brother is crying. He asks Lil E what's wrong and a crying Lil E responds by saying, "JR I don't want to go home. Can we just stay at school?" JR puts his arm around his brother and tells him that he has a plan, and they will be safe soon. JR plans on meeting with Lil Randy and Trey about making some quick money. They begin to walk home and as they get close to Troy's Chicken and Fish; JR and Lil E see police cars everywhere with several men and boys being loaded into them. As the cars pull off, JR sees a

51 | P a g e

Chapter 2 – Shorty Wanna Be A Thug?

very familiar face in the backseat of a car, Lil Randy. With tears in his eyes Lil Randy nods his head at JR as the police car he is in rides by. JR looks up and sees Trey standing across the street. Trey screams out, "Hey JR we just got a job opening. It's yours if you want it." After seeing Randy in the back seat of that police car, JR's dreams of becoming a drug dealer disappear instantly. He and Lil E begin to run up the block and head to the park to shoot basketball.

Once at the park they see Willie sitting on a bench by the court drinking a beer. He gets up and grabs the basketball from JR's hands and says, "I see your lil homeboy finally got busted. Stay away from those older clowns up there. They will all end up dead or in jail." JR says, "I don't like those dudes anyway." Willie says, "Whatever, I see how you look at them and their money and cars. Let's make a deal. If you stay away from Trey and his crew, I will stay sober and meet you every day after school to show you how to really shoot some ball." JR is smiling from ear to ear and says, "It's a deal." Lil E runs to the swings while Willie and JR go through some basketball drills. Before they realize it, several hours go by. JR says to Willie, "I have to go home. My mom is going to kill me." He grabs his ball and backpack and yells for Lil E to come on and they both run home.

JR and Lil E make it home and are greeted by their mother standing in the doorway. She screams, "Where in the hell

Chapter 2 – Shorty Wanna Be A Thug?

have you been. It's 7 o'clock." Before JR can respond she slaps him. As he cries, he says, "I was at the park shooting hoops with Willie. He's helping me with my game. He says I can go to the NBA if I work hard enough." "So, you're taking advice from a whino? You just need to focus on your schoolwork. Now get your ass in the house and eat dinner" says his mother. Before she can close the door Willie appears and says, "Sorry for having him out so late. It's all my fault. It won't happen again." Before she can respond Big E comes to the door and says, "You damn right it won't happen again because he won't be hanging with your bum ass. Now get the hell out of here." He then slams the door in Willie's face. He goes to the back and gets JR and grabs him by the arm and says, "Stay away from that bum ass clown. And by the way, I heard that your boy Lil Randy got locked up today, so Trey has a job opening. Instead of shooting ball after school your lil ass will be getting some paper working for Trey." JR yells, "No I'm not. Now get your damn hands off of me." Big E shoves JR to the ground and kicks him in the stomach. Tee Tee slaps Big E and says, "Don't you ever touch my child again. Get your shit and get out." This is the first time she has ever stood up to him and this is also the first time he put his hands on one of her children. Big E laughs and packs a bag and leaves but not before punching a hole in the wall. However, he will soon be back. This would be one of many times that he leaves and is welcomed back by Tee Tee. Tee Tee gets on the floor with JR and rubs his head and says, "Baby it will be ok. Don't cry. You can shoot ball with Willie everyday if that makes you happy. Just make sure you are home by 6 pm. Is that a deal?" As he cries JR says, "Yes momma, it's a deal. Thanks. I love you." She then goes down the hall to find Willie to let him know that it's ok for JR to play ball with him after school. She knocks on the door and Willie answers holding an ice pack on his eye. She says to Willie, "What happened?" Deep down, she knows that Big E probably did something to him. A shaken Willie says, "You know damn well what happened. That crazy ass boyfriend of yours came down here and hit me and told me to stay away from JR, which is exactly what I'm gonna do." She says, "I am so sorry. JR is really excited about shooting hoops with you, and I want you to work with him. I'm afraid he's gonna start hanging with the wrong crowd. Please let me make it up to you. You can come and have dinner with us. I have some chicken from Troy's." Willie politely declines the dinner offer and agrees to continue to shoot ball with JR after school each day. She gives Willie a hug and a kiss on the cheek and heads back to her apartment. As she walks away Willie says, "Thanks. You tell him to be at the park at 3:30 sharp. I'm not going to wait around for him either." He's really bluffing because he knows he needs this just as much as JR does. She smiles and runs to tell JR the good news.

Chapter 2 – Shorty Wanna Be A Thug?

JR can hardly sleep that night. He is so excited about finally having someone to shoot ball with and not to mention he is also worried that Big E may come back and ruin everything. The following morning, JR is up much earlier than usual. He irons clothes and gets himself and Lil E dressed. He then fixes them both a bowl of cereal. His mom wakes up later than normal and jumps out of bed and rushes out of her room only to find her normally hard to wake children fully dressed sitting on the couch watching cartoons and eating cereal. JR says, "Ma I got this. I'm going to help out more around here. You can go back to bed." She smiles at him all the while thinking she doesn't know how she will manage with Big E out of the picture. Over the next couple of years JR's life consists of playing basketball almost daily with Willie, schoolwork and taking care of Lil E since his mom has to take extra hours at work with Big E gone. He makes straight A's, and the schoolwork is almost too easy for him at times. He also works at a barbershop sweeping hair on the weekends for a free haircut for he and Lil E and twenty dollars that he always gives to his mother. Although JR is content with his life with Big E gone, things are still tough for his family. His mom struggles to keep up with the bills and almost monthly, she gets a warning letter about late rent as well as cut off notices from the utility company. It is even harder having two kids that are growing so quickly. JR is now twelve years old, five foot seven and one hundred and fifty-five pounds.

As the end of the summer approaches, JR begins to get more and more nervous about starting the seventh grade. He figures that he will no longer be one of the biggest kids in school and he thinks he will have to deal with the older kids making fun of him. Once school starts his assumptions are absolutely correct. Almost daily, someone comments on his small clothing and dirty shoes. Looking forward to basketball tryouts, which are less than a month away, is the only thing that keeps him from losing it. His goal is to make the basketball team and hopefully that will get the kids off his back. He still works with Willie daily and he has gotten a lot better. He still does not think he is good enough to play with the best ball players in the neighborhood, so while they are inside the center playing, he plays outside with the older neighborhood guys. Most of the guys he's playing against are drunks and small-time drug dealers. The games have to stop occasionally for someone to take a swig of liquor or because a junky comes up wanting some drugs. A few of them are like Willie and have been playing basketball their entire lives and had dreams of making it big, so JR is actually getting better by playing against them. Sometimes the guys get a little rough with him and Willie has to step in to take up for him. One day an older guy elbows JR in the ribs as he drives to the basket. JR

Chapter 2 – Shorty Wanna Be A Thug?

drops to the ground and begins to cry. He gets up with tears in his eyes and walks off the court. All the older guys are laughing as he heads towards the street. One of the men yells, "Take your lil punk ass home." All the other men laugh. Willie runs behind him, grabs him by the arm and says, "Where the hell do you think you are going? If you keep walking, we are done mane. You can't just quit because someone does something you don't like. Man up JR. If you quit now, you will be quitting for the rest of your fucking life. Look at me. I quit. I gave up and now look at me. You can and will be better than me. Just don't give up lil man". JR wipes the tears from his eyes and heads back to the court. The older men all start clapping and laughing. One man says, "Aww that was sweet. Now bring your lil ass back out here. My bad for that elbow lil man. Now play ball and quit all that crying." He gives him five and pats him on the head. All of the other men come over and do the same. From that day forward JR never quit again. His days consist of nothing but school, shooting ball and helping his mother out around the house. The older guys notice he's getting better and give him more and more confidence with their praises. One man says to JR, "Hey lil man, when you gonna stop playing with us old scrubs and try out for the school? You ready now mane." Before JR could answer, he hears a voice from the sideline ask, "Yeah when are you going to try out for the school? You got game mane. Come here and let me holla at you." JR turns around and sees that it's one of the drug dealers from the neighborhood named Big Scott. He's a tall heavy-set dark-skinned guy that's always laughing and joking. He tries to keep the kids in the neighborhood out of trouble. He especially tries to keep Trey away from JR. JR says, "Yes sir Mr. Scott. Tryouts are in two weeks." Big Scott reaches in his pockets and pulls out a huge wad of money. He peels off two one hundred dollar bills and extends his arm to hand them to JR and tells him the money is for a new pair of shoes. JR says, "Thanks Mr. Scott but I can't take your money. My mom would kill me if I came home with some new shoes." Big Scott says, "Come on little man take the money. You need to get some new kicks and some shorts for the tryouts. Can't be out there looking like a bum. Them buddies you got on might blowout hooping with them boys." They both laugh as JR reluctantly takes the money. Big Scott says to JR, "Come to me if you or your momma need anything. I don't want you running around with these knuckleheads around here. You're smarter than that." He and JR fist bump and Big Scott walks away and gets into his Mercedes and drives off. Willie comes over and asks JR what he and Big Scott were talking about. JR doesn't say anything. He just shows Willie the money Big Scott gave him. Willie immediately says, "You can't take that money. Give it back to him tomorrow." JR says, "Come on Willie. Please. You don't have to hear the jokes they make about my shoes. If I show up to tryouts in some nice shoes, they may take me more seriously. Come on man. I won't spend it all and I will let you keep the change." Willie agrees and says, "You can keep the change. Keep your new gear at my crib so your momma doesn't find out about it." JR asks, "So can we go now?" Willie shakes his head, looks at his watch and says, "If we hurry, we can catch the bus downtown and be back before your momma gets home. They head up the street to the bus stop and catch the bus downtown so JR can pick out some shoes and basketball shorts. JR can barely stop smiling the entire bus ride. He clutches those two one-hundred-dollar bills like it's the last money on the face of the earth. Once they get downtown, JR goes to the shoe store while Willie and Lil E head down to get some peanuts and candy corns. JR has never been to a shoe store like this before. Where he gets his shoes, you go to the shelf and find your size, try them on and then buy the shoes. He just stands there with a confused look on his face as he looks at all the single shoes sitting on the displays. The salesman approaches JR and asks if he needs any help. JR says," Ummm yeah, I like those shoes right there, but they look too big." The salesman laughs and says," Is this your first time being in a shoe store like this? We got more in the back lil man. What size do you wear?" An embarrassed JR says, "I wear a ten." The salesman brings the shoes back and lets JR try them on. They are a pair of black, red and white hi-tops. Opening that box was like opening a box of gold to JR. He puts the shoes on, and he walks back and forth, jumps up and down and performs fake dribble and crossover moves in the shoes. After ten minutes the salesman comes over and says, "How do you like them? You're gonna be paying for them regardless if you like them or not if you keep running around in them like that." JR laughs and says, "I love them. I'm gonna be clean in these during basketball tryouts. Just need to get some socks, shorts, t shirt and a warmup suit. How much are the shoes?" The salesman tells JR that they are one hundred and forty-nine dollars plus tax. With a disappointed look on his face, JR looks at the two hundred dollars in his hand and just shakes his head because he knows that he will not be able to get all of the other items he wants. The salesman sees the frustrated look on JR's face and says, "Look lil man, today is your lucky day. I'm gonna hook you up. You can use my employee discount for the shoes, and I will throw in the socks, basketball shorts and a solid tee in for free. When you leave here, just head up the strip and there is a small shop that sells some nice warm up suits. Ask for Jay and tell him that Tony sent you and he will hook you up." JR says, "Really? Thanks sir. I won't forget this." The salesman laughs and says, "Mane don't call me sir. You just make sure you make the team and send me some tickets when you go to the NBA.

Chapter 2 – Shorty Wanna Be A Thug?

Now go pick out some shorts and a shirt. I got other customers."
JR picks out some socks, shirts and shorts and then checks out.
His total comes to a little under one hundred and fifty dollars.
He runs out the store to catch up with Willie and Lil E. After
finding Willie and Lil E at the candy shop, they all head to the
shop that the salesman told JR about. Willie asks to see the shoes
so JR hands him the bag. Willie says, "These shoes look
expensive, how did you get all of this and still have money for a
warmup suit? Your ass better not be stealing." JR says, "Relax
Willie, the guy at the store hooked me up." Willie looks at him in
disbelief, hands him the bag back and says, "Hurry up in the next
store, I'm tired as hell." Once they arrive at the next store, JR
immediately finds the display containing all of the warmup suits.
As he flips though the different warmups one of the salesmen
approaches him and asks if he needs any help. JR whispers, "Are
you Jay? Tony sent me." The salesman responds, "Yeah, I'm Jay.
But why in the hell are you whispering?" JR looks around and
says, "Tony told me that you would hook me up." Jay laughs
and says, "Man chill out with the whispering, I own this shop lil
man. We aren't stealing anything. Do you like the sweat suit
you're looking at? Man let me see your kicks." JR nods his head
to say yes and hands him the shoes. Jay holds the shoes up next
to the black and red sweat suit and smiles. He looks at JR and
says, "Boy you gonna be fresh as hell." JR smiles and asks if he

can try the outfit on. He runs to the back and tries the sweat suit on and comes out to model it for Willie, Jay and Lil E. Lil E gives his big brother a thumbs up and smiles. JR says, "Willie, what do you think about the outfit?" Willie just shrugs his shoulders and points to his watch to let JR know that he needs to hurry up. JR tells Jay that he is going to get the sweat suit. Although the sweat suit is listed at seventy dollars, Jay tells JR to just give him forty dollars and says, "If Tony sent you down here, he must see something in you. Keep doing what you are doing." As Jay is putting his sweat suit in the bag, JR asks, "So how did you make it from the block to owning your own store." An offended Jay says, "What the hell you mean lil man? I got my business how most black folks do. I had an idea, wrote a business plan and I went to the bank and got a loan. Most of us ain't criminals lil fella." JR says, "My bad, but it just seems like where I'm from all the guys doing good are in the streets." Jay says, "It's all good lil man. You learn something new every day. Just stay in school and out of those streets. Remember, most of those guys that are doing good now may end up doing not so good at some point." Willie grabs the bag for JR, and they all run to the bus stop. As JR stares out the window of the bus, he thinks about what Jay says to him regarding the streets. It's no different than the things Willie and his mom have told him, but it seems to mean more coming from a young guy that actually has something going for himself and didn't get it from being in the streets. JR falls asleep during the bus ride and is awaken by Willie once they reach their stop. As they head up the block, they are stopped by Big Scott who is standing outside his car in front of Troy's. Big Scott says," Let me see what you got lil man." JR hesitantly hands him the bag. Big Scott looks at the outfit and shoes and smiles and says," Oh yeah, you gonna kill them with this boy. Now remember what I told you earlier. Gone head to the crib. Police are hot as hell out here." JR gets his bags and he, Willie, and Lil E all head to their apartment building. Once they make it to the sixteenth floor, JR hands Willie his bags to hide in his apartment and he and Lil E head to their apartment.

A few weeks pass and the day that JR has been waiting on finally comes. Boys Basketball Tryouts will be held today after school and JR is extremely anxious. He barely sleeps the night before and he's up two hours earlier than usual. For about thirty minutes, he paces around the living room with his basketball in his hand envisioning what he will do during the tryouts. He eventually wakes Lil E up, fixes them both breakfast, gets dressed and they both head out. His first stop is to Willie's apartment to change into his new outfit. He knocks on Willie's door and his knocks go unanswered. He beats on the door for what seems like an eternity before a half woke Willie finally opens the door. JR says, "What the hell took you so long?" A shocked Willie says, "You better watch your damn mouth boy. Your lil ass will be wearing what you got on to school." JR apologizes and walks into Willie's apartment to find his outfit laid out on the couch. JR grabs the clothes and runs to the bathroom to get changed. JR comes out the back sporting his new outfit and along with it, he's sporting a newly found confidence also. He grabs his backpack and basketball and he and Lil E leave out of Willie's apartment on their way to school. As he and Lil E walk up the block, they are greeted by some of the corner kids commenting on JR's new attire. "Damn JR you fresh ain't it, big shoe ass lil boy", one kid can be heard saying followed by laughter. Big Scott pulls up, rolls down the window and says, "I see you JR. Give them folks hell today lil man. Now y'all lil assholes quit playing and get to work." JR finally arrives at school and is greeted by the whispers of the boys in class talking about his outfit. One kid named Jamal, who is the starting PG on the basketball team, says, "Where you steal that from? Let me get the shoes before the police catch you with them on." JR says, "I will let you have them after I bust your ass today in basketball tryouts." Jamal and a few of the other guys that are on the team all laugh. Jamal says, "Your dusty ass trying out for the team? This should be fun. This bum thinks he can hoop. Tom Sheppard looking ass." None of the kids laugh at Jamal's joke. Jamal says, "So y'all don't know who Tom Sheppard is?

Chapter 2 – Shorty Wanna Be A Thug?

Y'all are some young lames." Before JR can respond, the teacher comes in and begins the day's lesson. The school day flies by and before he realizes it, JR is sitting in his sixth period class with 10 minutes before the end of class. The bell rings and JR hurries to the gym to get ready for tryouts. He changes into his basketball clothes, stretches and begins to shoot around. All the other kids eventually enter the gym along with the coach. The coach yells, "Starting five on this side and you in the yellow, you two big men, my man in the red and JR are skins." As JR takes off his shirt, he looks confused wondering how coach knows his name. He runs to half court to join the rest of his teammates. The coach tells them that the winner is the first team to score thirty-six points. The game starts and JR's team gets the ball first. They pass the ball into JR, he dribbles up the court and as soon as he crosses half court, he dribbles the ball off of his foot. Jamal picks the ball up and goes down the court and lays the ball up on JR. The next time down the court JR gets open and shoots an air ball from the three-point line. Jamal gets the rebound and comes down the court and hits a three on JR. After he makes the shot he laughs and says, "I thought you were gonna bust my ass Sheppard." Lil E screams, "Come on JR what are you doing?" JR smirks and nods at Lil E and begins to go to work. The next play down JR crosses Jamal over, drives to the basket and passes it to the center leading to an easy layup. Jamal, not to be outdone,

65 | P a g e

drives to the basket on JR but his shot gets pinned to the backboard by a high-flying JR. JR flies up the court and lays the ball up over the outstretched hands of the starting center. JR's team eventually wins the game, and he finishes with sixteen points, five assists, five rebounds, two steals and one block. Tryouts consist of a few more pickup games along with some drills. Once tryouts are over the coach calls JR over and says to him, "Don't bother showing up tomorrow." JR just looks at the coach with a puzzled look on his face and asks, "Why not? I know I started out slow, but I thought I played pretty good today. Come on, please give me another chance." Coach laughs and says, "Calm down young fella, let me tell you why you don't need to come back tomorrow. I've seen enough of you. You made the team." JR screams at the top of his lungs, "Yes, Yes Yes!!! Thanks Coach, but I'm coming tomorrow anyway. "Lil E brings JR his sweat suit, he gets dressed and they head out the gym. As they walk out the door Coach smiles and says, "Hey JR, tell my man Willie I said what's up." At that very moment JR realizes that's how Coach knew his name; Willie must have told Coach about him. JR and Lil E walks out the gym and much to their surprise sees Willie sitting in the hallway. Willie says, "I saw you doing your thang. You still got a long way to go though. Let's hit the park on the way home." JR says, "I just made the team and I just want to chill today. I'm too excited to work on

Chapter 2 – Shorty Wanna Be A Thug?

my game today. And by the way Coach says what's up. How do y'all know each other and are you the reason I made the team?" Willie says, "Me and Coach played together back in the day. I just told him to look out for you, but making the team was all you." JR turns around and says, "Willie, I will see you later. My mom is off today, and I can't wait to tell her that I made the team. Come on Lil E." As JR and Lil E take off running, Willie screams out to them, but they are too far down the hall to hear him.

    JR and Lil E makes it to their apartment building, runs up the sixteen flights of stairs and dashes to their apartment. They bust through the door to find JR's mom sitting on the couch watching TV. An excited JR says, "Mom I made the team." She just sits there and stares at JR. Lil E says, "Mom did you hear him? He made the team." She says, "Boy shut up and go to your room." JR stands there with a confused look on his face as Lil E goes into the bedroom. Once the bedroom door closes, she says, "Where the hell did you get those clothes?" In JR's rush to get home to tell his mom about making the team, he forgot to change out of the clothes that Big Scott bought him. It then occurs to him that must've been what Willie was yelling to him as he ran away. JR says," Big Scott bought them for me. He wanted me to look good for the tryout." Before she gets a chance to respond, she is interrupted by a knock on the door. She turns the JR and says, "We are not done boy." She opens the door and finds Willie leaned over and breathing heavily. She says, "What the hell do you want?" Willie gathers himself and says, "I'm coming to tell you about the outfit that I bought for JR." You talking about the outfit that JR just told me some drug dealer bought him Willie? Tell me more about it", she replies. Willie looks at JR shaking his head and says," Boy you can't hold water. Got me running three blocks to lie for you." Tee Tee says, "That shit is going back tonight. What's gonna happen when Big Scott asks you to do something to pay him back for that outfit?" JR walks into the room with his head down to take off the outfit. Willie looks at Tee Tee and says, "I know it's none of my business, but Big Scott is a decent guy. He just wants JR to stay out of the streets. He bought him that outfit just so he wouldn't get picked on during the tryouts. You should've saw him today. Your boy is good. He's smart too so he won't get caught up in the streets." Tee Tee says, "You know what you are right, it's none of your damn business. Now get out." JR comes out the bedroom with the clothes and shoes in a bag and with his backpack on. He says, "Ma I'm about to head to the laundry mat to wash these clothes. I will do my homework while I wait on the clothes to finish. See you later." He gives her a kiss on the cheek and heads towards the door. As he opens the door she says, "Boy come back here and put those clothes in the room. You can keep them. But don't make it a habit getting stuff from those damn drug dealers." JR runs back over and gives his mom a hug and heads back to his bedroom. However, this wouldn't be the last time Scott gives JR and his mom gifts. Tee Tee begins to depend on his help from time to time to keep JR and Lil E in some decent clothes. The following day JR is treated like a celebrity. He sees Big Scott as he leaves his building, and he is met with a handshake from a hand that was holding five one-hundred-dollar bills. JR says, "I can't take your money. I already got in trouble over the outfit." Big Scott says, "Don't worry lil man, I will talk to Tee Tee for you." JR reluctantly takes the money. Later that day Big Scott convinces Tee Tee that its ok to take money from him. He didn't want anything in return. He just wants JR to succeed because he's such a good kid. Everyone has heard that JR made the basketball team and as he and Lil E head to school everyone in the neighborhood congratulates him. He is greeted with high fives and fist bumps from the time he walks out the door of his apartment all the way to the school's front steps. All that changes once he sets foot into homeroom. As soon as he walks into class Jamal says, "Where's your new clothes? I see your lil dusty ass turned back into a pumpkin at midnight." None of the kids laugh at Jamal's joke. Jamal looks around the room and says, "Y'all dumbasses have never read Cinderella? Mane forget y'all." JR fires back, "You will have plenty of time to read fairytales while your bum ass is sitting on the bench this season."

Chapter 2 – Shorty Wanna Be A Thug?

He then pulls out the money that Big Scott had just given him
and says, "And I can buy me some more clothes whenever I want
to chump." A chorus of "Oooohs" can be heard coming from the
classroom as all of the kids laugh at JR's joke. Before they can
continue going back and forth, the teacher comes into the
classroom and all the kids take their seats. Jamal mouths to JR,
"You not getting my spot sucker." Jamal can't be any further
from being right, because once tryouts are over, and the season
starts, JR is the starting PG for the team. Things start out slowly
but eventually JR's team becomes one of the best teams in the
state. In his eighth-grade year, they lose in the championship
game when they had previously never made it to the playoffs.
His play lands him a spot on the Varsity team his freshman year
when freshman typically only play Junior Varsity. JR continues
to excel both in sports and academically and with the extra
money that Big Scott gives him occasionally he is able to help his
mom out, so everything is going great for him, Lil E and Tee Tee.

Early one morning as JR and his family are asleep there is
a knock on their door. Tee Tee jumps and screams JR get the
door. That better not be that damn friend of yours. He's getting
on my nerves always coming over so early. JR gets up and
answers the door and says, "What's up Jamal, mane you starting
to come here earlier each day." Although JR and Jamal start out
as bitter rivals, they eventually become best friends throughout

the course of them playing together. Jamal was moved to the
shooting guard position after JR took over the Point Guard
position. He was a better fit at two guard and he, just like JR,
ended up getting a position on the varsity team as a freshman.
Jamal says, "Mane you know the early bird gets the worm, now
get dressed so we can get some shots up before homeroom." JR
wakes up Lil E and they both get dressed and they all head to
school. As they are heading up the street a voice can be heard
saying," Hey what's up superstar?" JR turns around and sees a
tall skinny kid with braids in the shadows between two
buildings. The kid says, "What's up, so you don't remember me
superstar?" JR says, "Lil Randy, is that you mane?" He comes
from in between the buildings, and they shake hands and give
each other a big hug as JR asks, "So when did you get out and
what the hell are you doing up so early? You headed to school?"
Lil Randy responds by saying, "I've been out a week or so. And
to answer your other question, I'm just out here getting it how I
live." JR looks at Lil Randy with a confused look on his face. Lil
Randy says, "Mane don't give me that look, this is all I know. I
will be alright." JR says, "Dude you just did three years because
of this BS. Come on mane think." Lil Randy responds by saying,
"Boy you sound just like my uncle preaching to me from jail.
Y'all want me to get a job? Doing what? Go back to school? I'm
fifteen and ain't made it pass the fifth grade. They don't teach

Chapter 2 – Shorty Wanna Be A Thug?

you shit in there but how to survive in there. It's all good though fam. Thanks for worrying about me, but I'm good. And before I forget, I owe you an apology for trying to drag you into this bullshit. These dudes out here don't care nothing about you. All they care about is getting money. Peep this, when I got out, I asked Trey to give me a stack or so to help me get back on my feet. He told me I need to work for it and now I'm back out here. Do you believe that? I did that time when all I had to was tell on that fool and I could've been out. Enough of my bullshit mane, keep balling and going to school. That goes for you two funny looking dudes also." JR laughs and says, "Ok, I gotcha. I don't have practice today so when I get out of school let's go to my crib and play video games like we did back in the day." Lil Randy looks around and says," Yeah, if I'm still out here when school lets out. It's crazy out here. Now y'all get the hell out of here, I got work to do." As they walk up the street Jamal being the smart aleck that he is says, "So who is that depressing ass dude? Damn he put me in a bad mood. That boy needs a hug or something." JR says, "He's cool man. He once was my best friend before the streets got ahold of him and he got locked up. He's been through a lot so cut him some slack."

JR, Jamal and Lil E all go the gym and shoot around until school starts. While they are shooting around Coach comes in the gym and lets them know that they will be having a scrimmage

Chapter 2 – Shorty Wanna Be A Thug?

tomorrow after school. The Junior Varsity Team will play the Varsity team. He informs JR and Jamal that they will be playing with the JV Squad since they are both freshmen. After receiving that news JR can't wait to tell Lil Randy about the game. He's anxious to show him how good he's gotten at playing basketball. As soon as school is out JR, Lil E and Jamal all head to their apartment. On the way there they look for Lil Randy. He isn't in the same spot that he was in earlier, so they make a detour and head pass the playground to see if he's there. As they go around the corner they see police cars, ambulances and people gathered all around. Yellow tape surrounds a section in the corner of the fenced in basketball court. In the middle of the detectives JR sees a white sheet covering what appears to be a body. As JR makes his way through the crowd, he sees a familiar face up front crying and being held back by several people. It's Randy's mom. JR pushes his way to the front and in a concerned voice says, "What's wrong Ms. Pam?" She reaches over and hugs JR and says, "They are saying that's my baby Randy under that sheet." Tears roll down JR's face as he tightly hugs her back. With his head down, he slowly walks back through the crowd until he reaches Jamal and Lil E. Jamal says, "What's going on bruh?" JR places his hand on Lil E's head and says, "Man that's Lil Randy under that sheet. Shit is fucked up." Jamal puts his arm around his shoulder and says, "I'm sorry, come on fam, let's head to your crib and chill." As they head to their apartment, they overhear all of the neighborhood gossip about what happened to Randy. Word on the street is that Trey killed Randy for coming up short on some money and for talking about how Trey isn't loyal to his workers. This is partially true, Trey didn't kill Randy, however he got one of the young kids from the neighborhood to do it for him. The kid got caught a couple of hours after doing the shooting, but he never admits that Trey put him up to it. He never turns on Trey and instead he tells the police that he killed Randy over an argument during a dice game. Once they make it to the apartment, Lil E goes to the fridge and gets JR a drink and Jamal starts the video game. He throws JR a controller and they begin playing the basketball game. Five minutes into the game JR begins to cry and screams over and over, "I'm going to kill that motherfucker." His mom walks in the apartment as he is screaming and yells, "Boy what is your damn problem? Watch your mouth in my house." JR gets up and hugs his mom and says, "They killed Lil Randy. Everyone is saying Trey did it." She says," Oh baby I am so sorry to hear that. Baby, you can't stoop to their level. Let the police handle that. You just keep on doing you. That's how you pay them back by getting the hell away from them and never looking back." As they are talking there is a knock at the door. Tee Tee opens the door and it's Big Scott. He asks if he can come in to talk to JR. As he walks pass, he hands Tee Tee a couple of hundred dollars. Tee Tee wouldn't accept the money at first, but she needs it, so she eventually starts accepting the money. He sits down next to JR and puts his arm around him and says, "That was some foul shit that happened to your boy today. I know you're pissed off and want to do something about it but that's not you lil homie. I gotcha, you just stay out them streets. Don't throw your life away for those fools." JR nods his head and gets up and goes to his bedroom and doesn't come out until the following morning.

The following morning Tee Tee comes in the room and screams, "Y'all get up. Y'all are gonna be late for school." JR wakes up and says, "I'm not going to school today. I'm tired." She snatches the covers off of him and says, "Boy get your ass up. You're going to school. And you got a game today that I will be at. You don't go to school you won't be playing." That was enough to convince JR to get up and get ready for school. Before leaving the house, he gets a marker and writes RIP Lil Randy on both of his shoes. Lil E stares at him as he finishes and reaches his hand out for the marker. He then writes the same thing on his sneakers. JR spends most of the school day daydreaming, thinking about the game later and sleeping. His teachers are aware of what happened the previous day, so they all cut him some slack. The game is held immediately after school, so after their last class , JR and the rest of the basketball team head to the gym to get dressed. As they come out the locker room, JR looks in the stands and is surprised to see plenty of people from the neighborhood in the crowd. He sees his mom and Big Scott and several people wearing shirts that have RIP Lil Randy written on them. It takes all of the strength in him not to cry. His sadness quickly turns to anger once he sees Trey standing by the gym door. They briefly make eye contact and they both exchange head nods. The game begins and the JV team wins the jump ball and JR dribbles the ball off of his foot and it rolls into the hands of Leon, the starting point guard for the Varsity Team. He takes the ball and lays it up for two points. As he heads up the court he whispers to JR, "Relax lil man." He's taken a liking to JR and he's grooming him to be the backup point guard on the team. Eventually JR calms down and he begins to play much better. Well, that's until he looks in the crowd and sees Big E sitting next to his mother. Big E has been out of their lives for a while and JR has no idea how he knew about the game. JR doesn't know this, but his mom has been talking to Big E for a few weeks. He started calling her from jail a few weeks prior to being released a day before the game. As usual, he claims to have cleaned his act up, but JR knows that he probably just needs a place to stay, and he will be back to his old tricks again. Although he finishes the game with 18 points 10 assists and 5 rebounds, he plays poorly from the time that he sees Big E in the crowd. Once the game ends, Leon comes to JR and says, "What happened out there lil man. You lost focus out there." JR is just staring into the crowd watching as his mom and Big E walk out of the bleachers. That's when it hits Leon what the problem is. JR has talked to him about Big E in the past. He puts his hand on JR's shoulder and says, "Good game, now come on mane. Coach is waiting on us in the locker room." As they all exit the bleachers, Big E taps Big Scott on the shoulder and says, "Let me holla at you for a minute. Tee Tee told me what you have been doing for her and the kids and I appreciate that, but now that I'm back in the picture your help will no longer be needed." Big Scott says, "It's all good fam. JR and your boy are good kids, and a little money can keep them out of trouble. Don't take this the wrong way, but you just got out. Where are you gonna get bread to make sure that they are straight?" Big E responds by saying, "They are both my boys and I know they are good kids. I appreciate the concern but with all due respect step the fuck off now." Big Scott says, "It's all good homie. Y'all be good. Be sure to let me know when you swallow your pride and need some food to swallow, homie." Big Scott and his homeboys then leave the gym. As JR walks out of the gym he is met by his mom, Lil E and Big E. Big E extends his right hand out to give JR a handshake and says, "Good game son." JR ignores him and walks past Big E and goes straight to his mom and Lil E. He grabs her by the arm and says, "What the hell is he doing here? He's gonna do the same BS he does all the time." She immediately slaps JR and says, "First of all, remember who the parent is, so watch your damn mouth. Second of all, I'm grown, and I do what the hell I want to do, so mind your damn business."   A shocked JR takes off running and heads to the park where he bumps into Willie. They talk about Randy, school and shoot ball until after dark.

Once JR makes it home, he is greeted by Big E and his mom sitting on the couch. JR walks by without speaking to either one of them and goes into his bedroom. Tee Tee gets up and heads into the bedroom after him. Before she can say a word JR says," Ma you know he's up to no good. You always take him back and he ends up doing the same nonsense. I just don't want to see you get hurt again." She doesn't say a word. She gives JR a hug and a kiss and walks out of his room. In the back of her mind, she knows that JR is right and unfortunately Big E eventually gets back to his old tricks. However, for a month he is on his best behavior.   Big E finds a job within a few days of getting out and is doing his part around the house. All of that changes once he reverts to his old habits; drinking, drugs and once again beating on Tee Tee. He eventually loses his job and begins using most of the money that's for bills and food on drugs and alcohol. Now that Big Scott is no longer helping out, they are in constant danger of getting the utilities turned off. Even though

Chapter 2 – Shorty Wanna Be A Thug?

her hours have been cut at the store, Tee Tee does manage to save enough money to always pay a couple of month's rent in advance. One day while headed to school JR sees Big Scott driving down the street and he flags him down. Big Scott backs his car up and pulls up to the curb. JR says, "What's up Big Scott?" Big Scott looks around and says, "What's up JR? What's good? "JR says, "Where have you been man? Are you no longer giving my mom money? We need help bad." Big Scott reaches into his pocket and pulls out a wad of money and counts out five hundred dollars and hands it to JR and says, "Now don't let your momma's crazy ass boyfriend find out about this. He told me not to give y'all anything else because he was back. I see that didn't last long." JR says, "Thanks and I'm sorry, I didn't know he told you that." That evening JR skips practice, like he's had to do several times recently for family issues, to give his mom the money he got from Big Scott. JR rushes into the apartment hoping that big E isn't home yet which he wasn't. He goes into his mother's bedroom, wakes her up and hands her four hundred dollars of the money. He keeps one hundred dollars for himself just in case his mom decides to give the money to Big E. She needs the money so bad that she doesn't even ask where it comes from. She thanks JR, takes the money and puts it in her purse and goes back to sleep. JR gives her a kiss on the cheek and goes into the living room to play video games. He skips practice often because he wants to be at home to be there for his mom and Lil E just in case Big E goes on one of his drunk and high rages. The coach has been lenient with him, but he is on the verge of being kicked off of the team as well as his grades have dropped drastically also. He falls asleep playing the game but is awaken by a commotion coming from his mom's room. She forgets to hide the money that JR gave her, and Big E finds it in her purse. He can be heard screaming, "Where the fuck did you get this money? It better not had come from that fat motherfucker Big Scott." Tee Tee doesn't respond. Big E takes the money and storms out of the apartment slamming the door behind him.

The following morning Tee Tee is getting ready for work as the kids get ready for school. Tee Tee is especially frustrated on this particular morning. Lil E is in one ear telling her that he's hungry and that he needs money for a school trip, while JR is in the other ear telling her that she needs to leave Big E alone. She can't take it anymore and when she thinks things can't get any worse, Big E comes in drunk, high and cussing. That's the final straw. She screams, "I'm sick of this shit. I can't take y'all bullshit anymore." She grabs JR by the arm and reaches in his pocket and pulls out a crisp one-hundred-dollar bill. She says," I knew your lil slick ass didn't give me all the money. I need to get away. I might just go stay with my cousin for a few weeks. Let y'all see how it is without me around here. Don't y'all call or come looking for me either." She pushes Big E out the way and rushes out the door and heads to work. The kids and Big E just stand there and look at each other in disbelief. JR and Lil E head out to school while Big E plops down on the couch and falls asleep. When JR gets to school, Coach Jenkins is sitting in his homeroom waiting on him. He grabs JR by the arm and walks him in the hallway and says, "Where the hell you been boy? Do you not want to play? If it wasn't for my boy Willie, I would've been kicked your ass off of the team. What's going on?" JR just stands there, shakes his head and doesn't say a word. Coach says, "So, you don't have anything to say? Speaking of Willie, what has my boy been up to lately?" JR finally responds by saying, "Like I've told you before Coach, I've been having a few family issues. Just give me a couple of weeks please. I will be back and ready to play. Oh, and Willie is doing alright, I will tell him that you asked about him." After school JR heads home to find Big E and Willie sitting on the couch sleep. Liquor bottles and drug paraphernalia are scattered around on the coffee table. JR lied to coach earlier when he asked about Willie. Willie relapsed a month ago and has graduated to drug use after hanging around Big E. JR asks the two of them if they have seen his mother. His question goes unanswered. He searches the small apartment for any signs of his mom with no luck. He eventually looks in his room and sees that his pillow is out of

Chapter 2 – Shorty Wanna Be A Thug?

place. Initially he thinks Big E and Willie have been in his room looking for money until he looks under his pillow and finds a note with his hundred-dollar bill taped to it. The note is from his mom and reads, "Sorry about earlier, but I've been really stressed lately. Take your money and get something nice for yourself. I just really need to get away for a few days. Once I get back, I promise things will be back to normal." JR smiles and takes the money and the note and put them both in his pocket. Little does JR know that it will be a little longer than a couple of days before he sees his mom again. JR uses the one hundred dollars that he has to make sure he and Lil E have something to eat for dinner each day. With JR not having to worry about his mom and Big E fighting on a daily basis, he begins going back to basketball practice. Before he knows it, a week goes by, and he hasn't seen or heard from his mom. He asks Big E if he's heard from her, and he lies and tells him that he talked to her the other day and that she was still at her cousins. JR begins to worry about his mom, and on top of that they are running low on money. He only has the ten dollars left from the one hundred dollars that he had when his mom left, and they received a cut off notice for the lights a couple of weeks before his mom left. The following day, after walking with Lil E to school, JR decides to skip school to look for Big Scott. Big Scott hasn't been seen in the neighborhood for about a week or so. JR walks for hours, visiting all of Big

82 | P a g e

Chapter 2 – Shorty Wanna Be A Thug?

Scott's normal hangouts and no one has seen or heard from him in a week. While heading back home he decides to stop by Troy's to get some wings for his lunch and for he and Lil E to have for dinner. Before he heads into Troy's he sees Trey pulling up. As much as he hates Trey, he walks over to his car to ask him if he's seen Big Scott. In typical Trey fashion he laughs and says," Yo, you ain't heard. Word on the street is that the last person he was seen with was your bum ass daddy. They said that crazy dude killed him and ate his fat ass. I heard he sold what he didn't eat to Troy's. Enjoy your lunch you lil asshole." Trey is always picking with the younger kids, especially JR since he won't come work for him. JR just shakes his head and walks into the restaurant. Before he can place his order Troy asks," Why ain't you in school boy?" JR lies and says, "I was sick this morning, so I didn't go. Hey Mr. Troy, can I get a twenty-piece wing with two orders of fries." Troy says, "I gotcha lil man and your total is seventeen fifty." JR reaches into his pocket knowing that he doesn't have enough money and pulls out the ten ones and counts them as if he doesn't know how much money he had. He acts surprised after counting the money in front of Troy. He then reaches into his back pocket as if he may have more money and that's when Troy stops him and says, "Just give me the ten. That will cover it lil man." While JR waits for his order, he asks Troy if he has any positions available. Troy responds by saying, "None for you, and if I did, they would be for the day shift, 10 am to 3 pm, times when you will be in school when you aren't sick. Your order is ready too." When JR gets to the counter to get his food he says, "Come on Mr. Troy, I really need a job so school will just have to wait. It's just me and my lil brother right now. My mom is sick and is in the hospital and you know about my crazy stepdad. Come on please, I need the money." When asked about his mom's whereabouts JR continues to use the story that she is sick and, in the hospital, because he doesn't want her to get in any trouble for taking a break from them. Troy thinks about it for a minute, and although he really isn't hiring says, "Mane make sure you show up tomorrow at ten and not a minute later. You will get seven dollars an hour." Without even knowing what he will be doing, JR says, "Thanks, Mr. Troy, I really appreciate it. You won't be disappointed. Hey, do you think you can give me an advance on my pay for a week?" Troy laughs and says, "Boy get your ass out of here before I change my mind." JR grabs his food and runs out of the store. JR, excited about his new job, rushes home only to find the lights have been turned off. He just sits down, eats a few wings and takes a nap before it's time for him to walk Lil E home from school.

The following morning JR gets up and walks Lil E to school. He stops about a block short just to make sure none of his teachers or coaches see him. On his way back from walking Lil E

Chapter 2 – Shorty Wanna Be A Thug?

to school he decides to stop by Troy's and wait until Troy shows up. While he waits up front, he starts cleaning up around the building. As he is cleaning Troy pulls up and yells out of the window, "Don't think I'm gonna pay you for cleaning up all that crap. You shouldn't have showed up so early. Should've saved it for later while you're on the clock." He gets out of the car and they both head into the building. On his first day, JR runs the register, washes dishes, delivers orders, busts tables and cleans up around the restaurant. He is such a hard worker that Troy has to remind him to take a break. Before he knows it, it's 3 o'clock and time for him to go meet Lil E to walk him home. Before he leaves Troy goes into the register and hands him some money and he also gives him some of the call-in orders that people never picked up. JR counts the money and says, "Not to put your counting skills on the spot but this is sixty dollars, it should only be thirty-five." Troy responds by saying, "You might be the smartest dummy I know. I paid you for the hours you worked before your official shift, and I gave you a small bonus for working so hard today. Don't expect this tomorrow though. I don't need you here until ten a.m. Now, once again, leave before I change my mind. When JR gets home, he hides his pay for the day, helps Lil E with his homework and enjoys the food from Troy's. This would become his daily routine for the next couple of weeks. He needs to save at least two hundred dollars to get the lights turned back on. One night while he and Lil E sat in the living room lighted by candles, they hear someone trying to get in the apartment. They both get excited thinking it's their mom but get a big surprise when it's the apartment manager followed by the police entering the apartment. The officers search the apartment and come back and show JR and Lil E a picture and say if you see this man call us immediately. The photo is a picture of Big E. Apparently, Trey wasn't telling a complete lie when he said that Big E had killed Big Scott. On the night that Big E took the money that Big Scott had given JR, he takes the money and goes out and gets high. While he's out, he runs into Big Scott coming out of the corner store and confronts him about giving JR money. Big E screams, "Yo, you fat motherfucker, didn't I tell you about giving money to my family." Big Scott laughs and says, "Mane get your junky ass out of my way before I slap the taste out of your mouth." Scott pushes Big E out of the way and starts walking to his car. As he is getting in the driver's side Big E comes from behind him and stabs him repeatedly in the back. He puts Scott in the trunk of the car and drives the car to an apartment complex where the car remains until the police discover it a week later. Big E's fingerprints are all over the car along with the knife which he left n the car also. After finding out what Big E did to Scott, JR is tempted to tell the officers about not seeing his mom for a few weeks. He fears that Big E may have done something to her also. He also fears that if he tells the police about her leaving them that she will get in trouble and they will be placed in foster care, so he says nothing and just hopes that she comes home soon. The next couple of days JR spends worrying about Big E showing up to the apartment. His fears come to an end when the cops find him hiding out in Willie's apartment two days after the cops come to their apartment. Big E is eventually sentenced to life in prison for the murder of Big Scott.

JR is relieved when he finds out that Big E is in jail, but now he must focus on getting the remaining money for the light bill today. He is only twenty dollars short, and he plans on asking Troy for the money early today so he can pay the bill during his break. The day begins like any other day does with him getting Lil E ready for school, stopping at the corner store to get a sausage biscuit hash browns and orange juice for the both of them, walking Lil E to school and then heading to Troy's. He sits out front as usual waiting on Troy to show up. As usual, Trey pulls up showing off his money and trying to get JR to join his crew. And as usual, JR turns him down. Troy shows up a little later than normal on this day and he is in an even grumpier mood than normal. JR playfully says, "Man you're late. I'm gonna have to dock your pay." Troy responds by saying, "Find someone to play with boy. Today isn't the day for your jokes.

Now let's get to work." Things are pretty tense for the next hour
with JR trying to avoid getting in Troy's way. He finally builds
up enough confidence and says, "Mr. Troy, do you think I can get
twenty of my pay now so I can go down and pay the light bill for
my mom so we can get our power turned back on?" Without
looking up, Troy says, "Yeah kid, go in the register and get the
entire thirty-five I owe for the day. You can take your time
coming back." JR goes into the register and gets the money and
heads to the electric company, which is a ten-minute walk from
the store, to pay the past due amount needed to get the power
restored in the apartment. After leaving the electric company JR
runs over to the apartment to make sure the lights are working.
The elevator is out again in the building, so he rushes up several
flights of stairs, runs down the hall and busts into the apartment
and immediately flips on the light switch. Much to his relief the
lights turn on. He plops down on the couch and smiles. He then
goes under the couch to pull out an old video game system that
he's hidden from Big E. As he goes to hook the video game
system up to the small television in the living room, he notices a
letter on the coffee table. It's an eviction notice, that reads they
are behind a couple of months on rent and a total of one
thousand dollars needs to be paid by the end of the week or they
will be put out on the street. The money he just spent on the
lights could've gone towards the rent, but he was unaware that

his mom had trusted Big E to take care of the rent using the money she had saved. He took the two months' worth of rent money and bought drugs with it. JR unplugs the small television and places it in a box along with the video game console and the one game that he has. He figures he can get at least seventy-five dollars for them together from the pawn shop. He heads out of the apartment to go back to Troy's. On his way back to work he tries to think of ways he can get the rent money legally. All he can think of is asking Troy if he can give him an advance on his pay. When he gets back to work Troy, sitting alone behind the register says, "Damn boy you back already?" JR says, "It's one o'clock, I've been gone for a whole hour. Mr. Troy, can I ask you for a big favor?" Troy responds by saying, "I paid you for the whole day, there was no need for you to come back here to finish your shift. Well before you ask me for any favors, I got some bad news for you. The restaurant is doing bad and I'm going to have to let you go for a while. When we start back doing better, I can hire you back, but for now I have to let you go. Sorry little man. I packed you up a few to go plates. You probably don't want to ask me for that favor now do you?" JR grabs his food, shakes Big Troy's hand and thanks him for the food and the job and heads out of the restaurant. On his way out he walks by Terry and gives him a head nod to say what's up. When he gets outside, he sits on the steps of the restaurant to think about how he's going to get enough money to pay the rent. As he sits there eating wings, Trey pulls up and hops out the car up to his normal tricks. At this moment JR isn't mad at all about seeing him. Trey says, "Are you on your break or something? This stoop is reserved for my employees." JR says "Nope, I just got laid off. Are y'all still hiring? I need a job ASAP." Trey looks up the block and sees one of his people getting put in cuffs and thrown in the backseat of a police car and says, "A career opportunity may have just become available. It looks like one of my employees is taking an unexpected leave of absence. Today might be your lucky day." Trey goes over all of the dos and don'ts with JR and tasks him with soliciting customers, collecting the money and directing them to get the drugs from another kid up the block. After receiving his training, JR sits his food down and begins to work. Fifteen minutes go by and not one person comes through until Terry exits the restaurant. When he sees Terry, a nervous JR, with his voice quivering says to Terry, "Are you straight? What are you looking for?" This is the beginning of JR and Terry's encounter which ends with Terry telling JR to stay in school and to stay out of the streets.

Over the next couple of hours JR solicits customers and collects money from them and directs them to another kid down the street to get the drugs they've purchased. In just a matter of two hours, JR has twenty-five hundred dollars. This is the most money that he has ever put his hands on. Although he's only getting paid seventy-five dollars for the day, he feels good having that much money while barely breaking a sweat. He thinks he can get used to this line of work. Trey rides by every hour or so to collect the money from JR. Time flies by and before JR realizes it, it's four o'clock. JR has totally forgot about going to meet Lil E to walk him home from school. Before he can ask Trey if he can take a break, an angry Lil E comes running up the block screaming, "Where the hell have you been JR. I waited an hour for you. What are you doing out here?" JR says," Lil Bruh, I'm sorry, I was working and lost track of time." Lil E responds sarcastically, "Working? Looks like you're out here selling drugs, something you said you wouldn't do." JR says, "Look mane, I gotta do what I gotta do until mom comes back. I got the power back on today, so take this food and head home. By the time you finish your homework I will be home to kick your ass on the video game. Is that cool?" They give each other dap and a hug and Lil E heads home and JR continues to solicit people walking past the restaurant. A few hours pass and JR hears a commotion coming from the front of Troys. He peaks around the corner and sees Trey and another man arguing. Although he tries hard, he isn't close enough to hear what they are talking about. JR waits about five minutes after the man walks away, before he builds up enough courage to come over to Trey to say, "Yo Trey, what's

going on? Who was dude?" A surprised Trey says, "You don't
know who that was?" JR says, "No, should we be worried? Is he
coming back?" Trey laughs and says," Nah we good lil man, now
get your lil scary ass back to work." JR walks down the street to
solicit more people only to return to talk to Trey five minutes
later. Trey says, "What is it now?" JR hands Trey the money he's
collected and says, "Can I get paid so I can go home?" Trey
laughs and says, "You get paid once the shop slows up for the
night, which could be eight o'clock tonight or it could be three in
the morning. Now get back to work. I see why Big Troy fired
you. We still got customers." As JR walks away, Trey flags
down another kid to come over to get some more drugs from
him. Before he can hand the kid the bag, cops come flying from
both ends of the street with their sirens blaring. They
immediately block Trey's car in. With a cop coming towards
him, JR takes off running down the alley next to the restaurant.
He jumps several fences as he runs through backyards. The cop
is still behind him as he makes his way down another alley. He
runs to the end of the alley only to discover that it's a dead end.
With nowhere else to run, JR begins to cry, and lays face down on
the ground waiting on the officer to come to arrest him.

Chapter 3
Can't Teach An Old Dog New Tricks?

Chapter 3 – Can't Teach An Old Dog New Tricks?

After leaving Troy's, Terry goes to the park and sits in his car and eats before heading back to work. Once back at work he's bombarded with more issues and pretty soon it's 7:30 pm. When he realizes the time, he undocks his laptop, throws it in his bag and runs out of his office. Before heading home, he rides around for a while thinking about the possibility of him and Stacy actually adopting a kid. The thought of being a father scares him to death, especially knowing how he once was and after getting asked if he wanted to buy drugs by the young man earlier. He rides through his old neighborhood to see if the young man he saw earlier was still out there with Trey. He wanted to talk to him again to hopefully convince him that the street life isn't something he should be chasing after. Before heading back to Troy's, he stops by a corner store in the neighborhood to grab a beer. There is just something about his old neighborhood that he can't let go of. He loves the people there and he wants to eventually start a business in the neighborhood along with building homes there. He goes into the store and grabs a beer from the cooler, a bag of skins and a black and mild. After he pays for his items, he walks out and as he heads to his car he looks back and sees a guy with a hoodie on coming from beside the building. He thinks the guy is about to try something, so he hurries to the car and as he looks back again, he realizes he recognizes the man. Terry says, "Thomas, is that

Chapter 3 – Can't Teach An Old Dog New Tricks?

you man? It's me, Terry. We were in Juvie together. We called you Black Bill Gates because you were always talking about computers. What have you been up to?" The man with a puzzled look on his face says," Yeah that's me. What's up mane. I remember you." The man with his hands in his pocket keeps looking around and finally says to Terry, "You done mane? If so step off. We can catch up later. I got some business to take care of." Terry, noticing the butt of a gun hanging out of Thomas' pocket says, "Yo fam, what the hell are you doing? You trying to go back to the penitentiary? Fam don't mess up your chance like this. Come on mane. How much you think you gonna get out of that store? If it's money you need, I got a hundred." Terry reaches in his pocket to discover that he only has twenty-five dollars on him. He gave fifty to the young lady this morning and he spent the other twenty-five on lunch and the items he just purchased in the store. Thomas looks at Terry and says, "Are you done? If so, step off because this don't concern you." Before Terry turns and walks away, he says, "Mane you're making a big mistake. Here, take my card, give me a call, I may have a job for you." Thomas says, "I don't have a phone. How can I call you?" Terry reaches in his pocket and hands him an old flip phone that he uses in case of emergencies. Terry says, "Call me fam, you're making a big mistake." Thomas watches as Terry makes his way to the car, he puts the hood back over his head and says," Yeah I know."

Fifteen years earlier, a fifteen-year-old Thomas sits at the kitchen table eating breakfast with his mom, dad and little sister. As he finishes his last piece of bacon, he looks at his watch and says, "Oh snap, I gotta go, I'm going to be late for school." He grabs his lunch and his backpack, gives his dad dap and his sister and mom a kiss and runs out the door. As he leaves the house his mom screams, "Don't be hanging with those damn thuggish friends of yours. I know they had you out late last night." He runs up the street and makes it just in time to catch the bus. Today is his first day of high school. He is greeted on the bus by three of his friends, Larry, Carlos and Eddie. He gives each of them five and sits down. During the bus ride to school, he and his friends talk about all of the things that interest them. Thomas talks about how he spent most of summer doing odd jobs to make money, so he could buy parts for a computer he built. The conversation quickly shifts from video games to comic books to sci-fi movies until Eddie interrupts and says," Y'all we have to chill with all the nerd talk. This is our first day of high school and I'm not going to be known as The Nerd Herd as they called us in middle school." This is definitely not the group of friends that his mom is referring to as thugs. She is talking about the other guys in the neighborhood that he associates with from time to time. They all laugh, and Thomas says, "Mane you know that name is funny, and you know that I will gladly whoop anyone that goes pass the name calling with us." Although Thomas is a very smart and good kid, he often finds himself in trouble due to fights with the occasional bully. Eddie, a much smaller kid, tells Thomas, "I appreciate your efforts, but I can't have you taking up for me all the time." Thomas says, "I gotcha, it's all good fam. Now come on mane, let's go into this new school and be stars." They exit the bus and head into the school and head into their homerooms. All four of them have the same homeroom teacher. They all look at their schedules to see how many classes they take with each other. Eddie, nervous as usual, is worried once he discovers that he is taking Algebra and he knows seniors will be in the class. Thomas says, "Mane relax, I'm in the same class. It will be a breeze. We probably know more than their dumbasses anyway. Just chill out sometimes." Once they leave homeroom, they all head to their first period class, which is Algebra, the class Eddie is nervous about attending. The algebra teacher, Mr. Jackson says, "Everyone please quiet down and take a seat. Now let me see where everyone is at so I can know where to begin our lesson.   Who can solve the problem I have on the chalkboard?" The problem is 6 + 4 – 6 * 4. After a minute of silence Thomas looks around and raises his hand and says, "Mane this is too easy. The answer is negative 14." Mr. Jackson says that's correct." Thomas gives his boys high fives as the older kids in class all scoff. One of the older kids says, "Mane how did I get 16?" Thomas laughs and says, "Because you are slick slow." Everyone in the class laughs except, Jason, the kid that Thomas was making fun of. When class lets out all of the kids make their way into the hallway. As Thomas jokes with his friends, the kid he joked on earlier comes from behind him and punches him in the back of the head. Thomas turns around and punches him repeatedly until he falls down. Thomas' friends pull him away before school security and the principal makes their way to the fight. The kid he fought gets up and screams, "This ain't over mane!" As they walk away Eddie says, "Mane you always got something to say. Dude is gonna get us." Thomas says, "Mane we are good now. No one will be messing with us after that ass whooping I put on him."

When school lets out, Thomas and Eddie head to the bus stop while the rest of their crew is staying after school trying out for the Chess Team. While waiting for the bus, a couple of guys from the neighborhood, Trey and Tyrone, pull up in a yellow two door Cutlass with twenty-two-inch rims on it. These are two of the kids from the neighborhood that Thomas hangs with that his mom refers to as thugs. They are always getting into trouble and are always in and out of jail. Tyrone yells out the window, "What's up Thomas? Get your ass in the car. Let's ride out."

Chapter 3 – Can't Teach An Old Dog New Tricks?

Thomas asks, "Where did y'all get this car? Who did y'all jack for this?" Trey says, "Man you know that's racist right? My older cousin let me keep the car. Now get in." Thomas says, "I got my boy Eddie with me, I'm going to hang back and wait on the bus with him." Trey says, "His lil lame ass can roll with us too." Eddie looks at Thomas and shakes his head telling him he isn't going to ride with them. Both boys quickly change their minds as they look up and see the kid from earlier and about five of his friends quickly approaching the bus stop to get revenge for the fight earlier. Thomas says, "On second thought, I think we will take you up on that offer for a ride." Eddie and Thomas both run to the car and get in. As they pull off, Jason and the group of kids run after the car cussing and screaming. While pulling a gun from under his seat, Trey asks, "Who are those fools? We can turn around and take care of that for you." Thomas says, "We are good. I just had to whoop that fool earlier today. It will be all good tomorrow." They drive for about fifteen minutes and Eddie begins to get nervous after noticing they aren't headed towards the neighborhood. Eddie says, "Mane where are you headed? I have to be home by 3:30." Trey says," Sit back and relax lil dude, we are going to get you home." Just as he says that, the police pulls out from a side street and gets behind them. Tyrone says, "Damn, the police are behind us. Everyone put your seatbelts on and don't look back. I can't go back to Juvenile." Thomas says,

Chapter 3 – Can't Teach An Old Dog New Tricks?

"What are you talking about? I thought you said this was your cousin's car." Trey says, "Well we lied, we stole this car last night. Now just chill." As soon as they put their seatbelts on, the police turn on their siren. Tyrone quickly makes a right turn and speeds off. The police give chase for about five minutes as they weave in and out of traffic until they crash into a fence. During the crash, the gun under Trey's seat slides to the back seat and sits at Thomas' feet. When the police approach, Thomas reaches and grabs the gun in an attempt to hide it, but before he can do anything the police have their guns pointed at them. He quickly grabs the gun and the police snatches all of them out of the vehicle. One of the officers screams gun, and throws Thomas to the ground. Thomas says, "That ain't mine mane. You put that in the car." The officer says, "Yeah right, you're going to jail. We will figure that out downtown." The police officers load the four boys in the back seat of the car. On the ride down, Eddie will not stop crying and talking about how his mother is going to kill him. One of the officers says, "Damn right she is going to kill you. You better start talking. That car didn't steal itself and that gun didn't come with it." Before Eddie can say anything, Thomas elbows him in the ribs and says," Just chill. We will be good. Ain't that right Trey?" He glances over at Trey and Trey turns his head and looks out the window of the car.

Chapter 3 – Can't Teach An Old Dog New Tricks?

Once at the police station, all of the boys are placed into a holding cell. Eddie is crying while Thomas just paces back and forth. Tyrone says," Y'all just chill and don't tell them nothing and we will be out of here. I've been down here too many times. I know the routine." Thomas asks, "Does the routine involve telling them what really happened so me and Eddie can go home?" Tyrone looks at Thomas and just shakes his head. A guard comes in to get the four boys so they can go see the judge. The judge says, "Young men, you are being charged with vehicle theft, evading arrest, possession of a firearm, two counts of robbery and assault. Your bond is set at fifty thousand dollars each. You each will get one phone call before being taken to your cells." Thomas screams to the judge, "What do you mean armed robbery and assault?' Trey, Ty what the hell is he talking about mane?" Trey says, "Mane shut the hell up." The gun that was found in the car was linked to a robbery and a shooting that Trey and Tyrone actually committed the night before after they dropped Thomas off at home. The four boys are all escorted to the phones to make their one call. Thomas calls home, and his mom accepts the call and says, "Boy what the hell are you doing in jail?" Thomas says, "Mom I swear didn't do anything. I was only in the car with Tyrone and Trey and the police pulled us over and found a gun, the car was stolen, and they are putting a robbery and shooting on us." She screams, "Why the hell were you in a car with those damn thugs? Did you miss the bus or something? I told your dumbass about hanging with those damn fools." A crying Thomas says," But I promise I didn't do anything. The judge says our bail is fifty thousand dollars and you just have to come up with ten percent of that. Can you please help get me and Eddie out of here?" His mom says," What do you mean you and Eddie? You got lil Eddie into this too? That boy is in foster care. They aren't going to get him out. Boy we don't have that kind of money. Sorry but y'all are just gonna have to stay in there until the court date. If you really didn't do anything the truth will eventually come out." One of the guards comes over and lets Thomas know that he has to end his phone call. Before hanging up his mom tells him that she loves him and will try to see what she can do to get him out. As he is escorted to his cell, he notices Trey and Tyrone aren't at the phones anymore and he sees them sitting in an interrogation room talking to detectives. He smiles thinking that they must be confessing to what they did. Once he gets to the cell, Lil Eddie is already there sitting on the bottom bunk crying. Thomas says, "Mane stop crying, we are getting out of here. I saw Trey and Tyrone talking to the detectives, so they are probably telling them we had nothing to do with any of this." Lil Eddie says, "Mane are you stupid?" Thomas says, "Mane watch your mouth. What are you talking about?" Lil Eddie says, "You really think those

Chapter 3 – Can't Teach An Old Dog New Tricks?

two fools are going to take the blame for this? What's this, like their tenth time going to jail? They are going to hide them if they admit to doing all of that stuff. Before my brother passed, he told me that the biggest liars and snitches are these so-called street dudes. Always throwing around not snitching and loyalty but will snitch on their momma to get out of trouble. For all we know they are telling them that you stole that car, robbed that man and I shot JFK and MLK. Mane, we are screwed." Thomas puts his arm around Eddie's shoulder and says, "They wouldn't do that. Those are my boys. We are going to be alright. We should be home in no time."

The following day while Eddie and Thomas are in the cafeteria eating, they see Trey and Tyrone come in. They make eye contact, and they both give a head nod to Eddie and Thomas as they proceed to get in line. Some kid comes over to Eddie and takes his hamburger. Thomas immediately gets up and hits the kid in his mouth. Three other kids quickly join the fight and Eddie and Thomas eventually fight them all off. Realizing Trey and Tyrone did not come over to help them, Thomas screams at them," Y'all just gonna watch them kick our asses like that?" When Trey and Tyrone get their food, they come over to where Thomas and Eddie are sitting. Trey says, "Mane we have priors, we can't be getting into any BS in here." Eddie looks at Thomas and says, "See I told you?" Trey says," What the hell does that mean lil dude?" Thomas says, "Mane don't worry about that. What were y'all talking to those detectives about? Were you telling them what really happened?" Tyrone says, "Damn fool, you think we are gonna tell on ourselves? These folks are gonna have to do their jobs. Nobody is admitting to anything. You just don't tell them anything." Eddie mumbles to himself, "Still didn't tell us what y'all were talking about with them folks." Tyrone says, "Bruh you got a smart mouth. What are you trying to say? You think we snitching? Say what you feel and get hit in the mouth lil dude." Thomas interrupts and says, "Look man we didn't do anything, and we just want to get out of here. We aren't gonna say anything but do what's right fam. Remember you said you would always look out for me." Tyrone and Trey both nod their heads and gives Thomas dap.

Three months pass and the boys are all still in jail. One day Thomas and Eddie are in the cafeteria and see no signs of Trey and Tyrone. Eddie says, "Where are your boys. Probably in the interrogation room eating a four-course meal, smoking a pack of cigarettes and playing video games." Thomas replies, "Chillout. They probably ate already and are back in the pod or they probably whooped some fool and are in solitary confinement." For the next month they have this same conversation during breakfast, lunch and dinner. Eddie says, "I know they are your boys and all, but I think they may have

Chapter 3 – Can't Teach An Old Dog New Tricks?

double crossed us. Where are they? We just need to tell the police what really happened so we can get out of here." Thomas says, "Just chill, I'm going to call my mom and dad next week and have them call the lawyer for us to see what's going on." Eddie says, "Look man, I have all the faith in the world in your moms and pops, but I swear I can't do another day in this place. I just want to go home." Thomas says, "I feel you. I gotcha man. Appreciate you being solid with this."

A week passes and there is still no sign of Trey and Tyrone. Thomas jumps off the top bunk and says to Eddie, "Get up, I'm about to head to the yard to ball on these boys." Eddie says," Go ahead without me. I'm just gonna chill and finish reading this book." Thomas says, "Are you sure? These fools might come in here messing with you. You always go with me. What's up?" Eddie says, "I'm good. I'm not worried about these fools anymore, and you can't be taking up for me all the time. Looks like we aren't going anywhere soon anyway so I have to learn to defend myself in here. I'm straight mane." Thomas, although skeptical, just shakes his head and leaves to go shoot ball. Thomas is a very good basketball player, but he always preferred being in the academic clubs over playing sports. As he always does, he's having his way on the court with the other kids and talking trash. And as he always does, he ends up in a fight. Thomas dunks the ball on one of the other kids and knocks him down and stands over him. As Thomas walks away the kid jumps up and hits Thomas in the back of the head with the ball. Thomas runs over, grabs the kid by his shirt and starts punching him in the face. He gets him down and kicks him repeatedly until some of the other kids break it up. After the fight the guards end rec for the day and all the kids are taken back to their pods. Thomas runs to his cell and immediately starts talking about what just happened. "Eddie I just had to whoop a fool during rec. He hit me with the ball so I..." Thomas pauses and says, "Who the hell are you? Where is Eddie? Get the hell out of here." There is another kid in the cell laying on Eddie's bed. The kid responded, "I'm Terry and I don't know an Eddie. I just got here today and was told that this was my cell." Before Thomas can respond, four boys come in his cell and start jumping on him. It's the kid he just fought on the yard and three of his friends. Terry jumps off the bed and helps Thomas fight the boys off. They eventually get them out of the cell. As Thomas catches his breath he says to Terry, "Thanks man. I'm Thomas. Sorry about earlier man. They must've transferred my boy Eddie to another pod." Terry asks, "Did he get in trouble or something?" Thomas looks confused and starts to wonder why they would transfer Eddie. He says to Terry, "Man he never does anything wrong. Something ain't right. I haven't seen the other two dudes I came in here with in three months. Now Eddie just disappears." Terry says, "Hate to be the one to break the news to you, but your boys might have flipped on you." Thomas just shakes his head and gets in his bed.

The following morning, as soon as the cell opens Thomas runs to the phones to see if he has money on his account to call his mom and dad. He places the call and his sister answers saying what's up big head. Thomas says, "Look, I don't have time to play with you. Where is mom and dad?" His sister says, "Why are you so mad? You should be happy since you are probably getting out soon. I saw your friend Trey and he said they don't have anything on you." Thomas screams, "Trey is out! What the hell. Put mom on the phone." She hands the phone to her mom. Thomas says, "Mom have you heard from the lawyer? I'm getting nervous." She says, "Yeah I talked to him. He will be up there to see you today. So, your wanna be criminal ass really did all of that stuff? The lawyer told me everything. Thomas says, "I didn't do anything." His mom screams. "Well, the lawyer says they have four witnesses that say you did this. He doesn't know who they are yet, but I bet it's Trey, Tyrone, Eddie and the man your dumbass robbed and shot. I can't believe you did this nonsense. You're just like the rest of these damn fools." Before Thomas can respond, she hangs up the phone. Later that day a guard comes into Thomas' cell and tells him that his lawyer is here to see him. Thomas is escorted to the visitation room. The lawyer stands up to let Thomas know who he is. The lawyer introduces himself to Thomas. His name is Carl Horowitz. Carl opens his briefcase and fumbles with a bunch of manila folders and pulls one out and says, "Ok Jason, we are going to get you out of here in no time. Indecent exposure isn't a major crime." Thomas says, "Man my name is Thomas and I'm in here for robbery, possession of a firearm and aggravated assault." Carl goes back into in his briefcase and pulls out the right folder. As he reads over the paperwork his eyes get big and he sighs and says, "Kid you need to just plead guilty. You can probably be out in five years with five years on supervised release. I will let the DA know you're going to plead guilty to see what they are going to offer." Thomas says, "Man I'm not doing five years. I didn't do anything." Carl sarcastically responds, "Yeah I know, you guys never do anything wrong. Kid they have four witnesses that are willing to testify that you had a gun and that you committed these crimes. There is nothing you can do but take a deal." Thomas says, "Man you are crazy. Who are these witnesses?" Carl responds, "This should come as no surprise to you, but the witnesses are your buddies, Grant Thomas III better known as Trey, Tyrone Perkins, Eddie Taylor and a kid named Jason Harding." Thomas puts his head down and starts to cry. He tells the lawyer, "Well I want to tell what really happened since they want to lie on me. And who the hell is Jason

Chapter 3 – Can't Teach An Old Dog New Tricks?

Harding?" The lawyer says, "Well kid, it may be too late for all that. Should've said something sooner. Now it's four against one. And I don't know who Jason Harding is other than someone that says you had that gun at school and bragged about robbing and shooting someone with it." The lawyer gets up to leave and says, "Young man, if you knew what was best for you, you would take a deal. I'm talking to the prosecutor in the morning to see what they will offer you for a guilty plea."

Thomas gets back to his cell and tells Terry what his lawyer said. Terry asks, "So what are you going to do? I know fools that have turned down deals and ended up getting way more time than they offered." Thomas says, "I'm not taking a deal. I didn't do anything except for get in the car with those damn thieving rats. Ain't no way these folks gonna send me to prison for something I didn't do." Terry laughs and says," Boy you got too much faith in the Criminal Justice System. They have been railroading brothers like us for years. How many years did he say he may be able to get you?" Thomas says, "He said he can get me five, but I can't do no five years for something I didn't do." Terry says, "Mane take them years. Five is better than fifteen. You probably won't go to trial until next year so that year you spend in here will count towards the five." Thomas looks at Terry and says," Whatever mane, ain't nobody asked you nothing anyway."

Chapter 3 – Can't Teach An Old Dog New Tricks?

The following day Thomas' lawyer comes back to visit. He tells Thomas that he got the prosecutor to agree to a plea deal that will require Thomas to serve five years. Two in Juvenile and the remaining three in an adult prison. Thomas screams "Mane I didn't do anything. I'm not accepting a deal. I'm trying to go to college to study computer science. I can't spend time in jail for something I didn't do." Carl says, "I don't care how innocent you claim to be. This is the best deal you will get. Going to trial is too risky and I can guarantee you that you will get the maximum twenty years if you are found guilty. Are you sure you want to do that?" Thomas screams, "I didn't do any of this stuff. I want to go to trial. I can let them hear my side of the story." Carl begins to pack up his things and before he leaves says, "Ok kid, I will let your parents know, but don't say I didn't warn you. Good luck." Later that day, Thomas makes a call to his parents. His mother answers and says, "I talked to the lawyer, and he told me your dumbass turned down the deal he got for you. What's your damn problem." Thomas says, "Can you put dad on the phone please?" His mom responds, "Oh ok then. Them folks gonna hide your hard-headed ignorant ass. When they give you all that time don't call me at all." His father takes the phone from his mother and says, "Son don't listen to her; she's just upset and disappointed in you. Now be straight with me man. Did you do any of that stuff they say you did?"

Chapter 3 – Can't Teach An Old Dog New Tricks?

Thomas says, "No sir and I'm not admitting to something I did
not do." His dad says, "Well son, if you didn't do it don't admit
to it. Just know that the punishment will be worse if you go to
trial and get found guilty. Either way I promise to be there for
you every step of the way." Unfortunately, he wouldn't be able to
follow through on his promise because his father passes away
before Thomas goes to trial.

After spending eighteen months in Juvenile Detention,
one week before his eighteenth birthday, Thomas' trial begins.
He isn't able to get a suit, so Terry's mom sent him one of her
brother's old suits to wear for the trial. Her brother is much
larger than Thomas, so the suit is much too big for Thomas. The
pants are covering his shoes and the coat comes past his hands.
Against his lawyers wishes, Thomas is escorted into the
courtroom handcuffed ankles to wrist. After he is seated, he
looks back to glance over the courtroom to see if he sees his mom,
but she holds true to her word and doesn't show up. He then
looks at the jury box and sees that the jury of his peers consists of
eight white women and four older white men. The judge enters
the courtroom, and the trial begins. During the opening
statement, the prosecutor refers to Thomas as a violent criminal
that needs to be locked away to protect the community and that
he has four witnesses that will all testify to his repeat criminal
behavior. Carl, Thomas' lawyer, stumbles through his opening

Chapter 3 – Can't Teach An Old Dog New Tricks?

argument without even mentioning two of the main witnesses' criminal past. He also never bothered to find out who the fourth witness was. His entire approach to this case, just like many of the cases he takes, was to get his client to plead guilty and take a deal. The prosecutor calls his first witness, Trey. When questioned, Trey admits that he and Tyrone stole the car, but he denies the robbery and shooting. He tells the jury that Thomas committed the robbery and shooting the night before they were caught in the stolen car. He says they only fled from the police because Thomas threatened to shoot if they stopped the car. Tyrone gets on the stand and repeats the same story that Trey told. After each one of them finished being questioned by the prosecutor, Carl declined to cross examine them. Thomas, whispers to his lawyer, "Why aren't you questioning them? They are lying. Aren't you gonna ask them about their records?" Carl sarcastically asks, "Who's the lawyer, you or me kid? No one cares about their little rap sheets. Now sit back and let me do my job." Carl did absolutely no research on Trey and Tyrone's criminal history. Any good defense lawyer would immediately point out that they are career criminals at the age of sixteen. The prosecutor's next witness is Lil Eddie. Eddie repeats the same story that Trey and Tyrone told. He says Thomas told him he robbed and shot a man and during the police chase Thomas kept yelling, "Don't stop the car. They are going to find this gun. I'm

111 | P a g e

Chapter 3 – Can't Teach An Old Dog New Tricks?

not going to jail for shooting that man." Once the prosecutor is done Carl decides to cross examine Eddie. His plan is to discredit Eddie by painting him as a disloyal friend that's lying on Thomas. Instead of the jury seeing Eddie as a disloyal friend, once Eddie starts telling stories about how Thomas has fought people to defend him most of his life the jury begins to see Thomas as a violent aggressive teenager that's capable of committing an armed robbery. The next mistake Carl makes is trying to blame Eddie for being the actual shooter. Had he done the least bit of research, he would've known that Eddie is in foster care and has to be in by 7 pm every night so he couldn't have committed the robbery which occurred at 9 pm. Once Carl learns that bit of information, he decides to not question Eddie any further. When Carl returns to the table Thomas says, "Mane what the hell are you doing? Eddie is a damn choir boy. He's only lying because they must've threatened him with jail time or something. Mane I swear I could've done a better job than you." The jury overhears the conversation, and you can hear laughs coming from the jury box. The judge says to Thomas, "Young man quiet down please or you will be asked to leave." Thomas tells the judge he will not disturb the courtroom again but that changes once the prosecutor calls his next witness. The prosecutor calls Jason Harding to the stand. As he is a sworn in, Thomas eventually realizes who he is and jumps up and screams,

Chapter 3 – Can't Teach An Old Dog New Tricks?

"What the hell is he doing here?" Jason Harding is the kid that Thomas fought on the first day of school. Carl grabs Thomas in an attempt to get him to sit back down. Thomas continues to yell, "I should beat your lying ass again sucka." The judge says, "Young man that was your final warning. Officers, please remove this young man from my courtroom." Thomas is forced to sit in a courthouse holding cell for the remainder of his trial. Jason goes on to testify that Thomas showed him the gun in class and told him that he robbed and shot a man the night before. He lies and says that their fight was over the fact that he told Thomas he was wrong for what he did by robbing and shooting someone. He even says that Thomas threatened to shoot him following the fight. After Jason's testimony both the defense and prosecution rest their cases. The jury deliberates for less than an hour before coming back with a guilty verdict on all charges: armed robbery, assault, evading arrest and auto theft. Carl goes to the courthouse's holding cell to give the bad news to Thomas. Thomas cries and asks, "How much time did I get?" To which Carl replies. "We will not know until your sentencing next week. But you should've taken that deal." The following week, on Thomas' eighteenth birthday, they are back in court for the sentencing. The judge gives Thomas a chance to speak to what he has done to which Thomas simply responds, "I didn't do any of that stuff your honor." The Judge says, "Young man, your constant courtroom disruptions, the fact that four of your friends all say that you committed these crimes and your lack of remorse for what you've done leaves me no choice but to sentence you to the maximum penalty of twenty years with parole eligibility after ten years. Good luck and may you come out a better person than you are going in as, which I highly doubt will be the case." Since Thomas is now eighteen, he is taken from the courtroom and immediately put on the bus headed to the State Penitentiary.

Prison is a lot different than juvenile for Thomas. There is way more violence in prison than there was in Juvenile. And he is no longer bigger than the other inmates so now he's on the losing end of most of the fights he's involved in early on in his bid. Fighting was an everyday thing his first couple of years. It was extremely difficult for him to get adjusted to prison life even though he had been incarcerated for almost two years prior. Some of the fights are due to Thomas just being angry about being locked up for a crime he didn't commit while others are due to the older inmates trying to take advantage of him by taking his lunch, keeping him from using the phone or pushing him around on the yard while shooting basketball. One fight in particular was the turning point for his life in prison. While eating lunch an older inmate comes over and grabs Thomas' orange and another grabs his sandwich and begins to walk away. Thomas jumps out of his seat and breaks the tray over one of the guy's head. With the sharp piece of the remaining tray, he cuts the other inmate's arm and begins beating him. When the guards intervene, Thomas hits one of them in the face and then tackles another guard. That fight lands Thomas in the hole for a little over two months. The time that he spends in the hole is what eventually transforms Thomas. All he hears in his head over and over is the judge saying that he hopes he comes out a better person than he went in as. So, after a couple of years, all of the fighting and bad behavior immediately comes to a complete stop for Thomas. Once Thomas gives up hope of being released early, he begins to just make the best of his time behind bars. Once he is released from the hole he begins to study for and receives his GED. He also eventually gets his Associates Degree in Information Technology and numerous technical certifications. He even gets a job working for the Bureau of Prisons Information Technology Department as a Helpdesk Technician for about twenty hours a week. When he's not working, he's in the Law Library or teaching basic computer courses to the other inmates and prison staff. His goal, once he's released is to get a job working in Information Technology and mentor youth on the importance of not hanging with the wrong crowd and eventually start his own IT consulting firm.

After spending years behind bars, the day Thomas has been waiting on finally comes. Thomas is released from state

Chapter 3 – Can't Teach An Old Dog New Tricks?

custody after serving a total of fifteen years; he spent three years in the juvenile facility and twelve years in state prison. Although he is ecstatic to finally be released, the moment is still bittersweet. No one is there to greet him as he is released since he hasn't heard from his younger sister or mother in a number of years. Upon his release he decides that he will not try to contact either of them until he gets on his feet. He doesn't want to intrude on anything they have going on. He only has two hundred dollars to his name and the clothes on his back, so the first thing he does is to try to find a job. Out of all places, the first place he calls is the prison he was just released from. He figures that since he worked there while serving time that he could definitely apply to get his old position back. He makes his way down the road to a payphone and calls the prison's helpdesk. One of the Helpdesk Techs answers and Thomas asks to speak to Antonio, the Helpdesk Manager. Antonio picks up the line and says, "Helpdesk, Antonio speaking. How may I help you?" An excited Thomas says, "What's up man, it's me Thomas." Antonio responds dryly with "Hi Thomas, how can I help you?" Thomas is surprised with his lack of enthusiasm being that they were cool during his time working for him. Thomas responds by saying, "Well man, I need a huge favor. I just got released today and I know that helpdesk position hasn't been filled yet, so I was wondering if I could get a shot at the position." Antonio laughs and says, "Are you serious?" An agitated Thomas says, "Why in the hell wouldn't I be serious? What's the problem?" Antonio says, "It's pretty simple, you have a felony, so we can't hire you." Thomas screams, "So me having a felony didn't stop me from working for you and doing a damn good job for fifty cent an hour? This is some BS and you know it. You are a real bitch for that. When I see you, I'm slapping the taste out of your mouth you clown ass sellout." Antonio laughs and says, "You might regret saying that and you just proved why we don't hire ex-cons." Thomas says, "Mane fuck you" and slams the phone's receiver down.

After the phone call with the prison, he makes the five mile walk to the nearest bus stop. His next destinations are to the halfway house to check in and then to visit his parole officer. After the hour-long bus ride, he walks a few blocks to the halfway house. He knocks on the door, and it's answered by the House Manager, Carlos Johnson. Carlos greets Thomas by saying, "Good Morning, I'm Carlos Johnson, the House Manager. And your name is?" Thomas responds by saying, "I'm Thomas. How's everything going?" Carlos says, "I'm good. Before you get settled in, let me go over the lay of the land for you. We have strict rules around here. You have to be here by eight pm unless your job requires you to work late, you must have a job, absolutely no visitors, no cussing, drinking or smoking and no

Chapter 3 – Can't Teach An Old Dog New Tricks?

fighting. Violating any of those rules can be grounds for being put out and potentially landing you back in jail. Now, let me show you to your room. By the way someone is already in your room waiting on you." A confused Thomas doesn't know who the man is sitting on his bed when he enters the room. The man stands up and says "Good morning, I'm Elliot Jenkins, your parole officer. I see you've had a busy morning, Thomas." Thomas just stares at him with a confused look on his face. Elliot says, "So you didn't threaten a man this morning less than an hour after being released from prison? Oh yeah, now you remember. A call was placed to the police stating that you threatened a man over a job. That can be considered a felony and could possibly send you back to prison. Good thing for you, when they contacted me about the altercation, I was able to reach out to the guy and have him chalk it up as just a simple misunderstanding between him and a frustrated ex-convict. However, one more mistake like that and you are going back. Since I've saved you a trip to my office to check-in, I expect you to immediately begin looking for a job." Thomas says, "I appreciate that, but dude was an asshole." Thomas looks over at Carlos and says, "I mean, he was a jerk."

After putting his belongings away, Thomas begins his job search. He uses the house computer to apply for jobs online. He spends a couple of hours online applying for everything from fast food restaurants to construction jobs to IT Helpdesk positions to call centers. All of the applications have one thing in common, they all ask the applicant if he or she has been convicted of a felony. A frustrated Thomas decides to just lay down and relax to enjoy his first day of freedom. Thomas sleeps from the afternoon until the next morning. He is awakened by Carlos at 8 am. Carlos says, "I see you got that first good night of sleep out of the way. That's normal. Some guys come in and sleep for a couple of days. Get up man. Take a shower and get out there and find a job. You need to be working by next week." A sleepy Thomas says, "Let me sleep for another hour or so. Wait what do you mean find a job by next week? No one is going to hire an ex-con." Carlos says, "That's not my problem. I'm not the one that robbed and shot someone. That's between you and the state of Tennessee." Thomas gets up, takes a shower, gets dressed and goes to the house computer to check his email to see if any jobs have emailed him. He's not surprised to find that the only responses he has are from jobs declining him due to his background. Thomas leaves the house, and his first stop is to visit his parole officer. After waiting in the lobby for about thirty minutes, he's finally called to the back. As soon as he gets to the back, he's handed a cup and told to go urinate in it. A surprised Thomas says, "Hey man I've only been out for a day; you really think I'm that stupid to go get high." His parole officer responds

Chapter 3 – Can't Teach An Old Dog New Tricks?

by saying, "You'd be surprised at how dumb some of you ex-cons can be." Thomas shakes his head and heads to the bathroom to pee in the cup and returns it to the probation officer. As the receptionist comes in and takes the urine sample, the probation officer says, "Take a seat. So, how's the job hunt going?" Thomas says, "Man I've only been out a day. I'm trying but it's tough being an ex-convict and all. Everyone that's responded to my online applications have said no due to me being a convicted felon." His parole officer says, "That's not my problem homie. But when you come here next week you better have a job and be prepared to give another urine sample. If these results come back dirty, don't even worry about coming back or finding a job, because you will be back in jail. Now have a nice day." Thomas says, "So that's it? No leads on jobs or nothing?" His parole officer says, "Does this look like a temp agency? As I said, have a nice day and close the door behind you when you leave. Thanks." Thomas leaves the parole office and catches the bus downtown so he can apply for more jobs. He goes from store to store filling out applications. On each application there is the question asking whether he's ever been convicted of a felony to which he answers yes. After turning in each application, the managers read over the application and sees that he's answered yes to being a convicted felon and immediately tells him they don't hire felons. The last place of business he visits he decides to no longer be truthful on the application and answers no to being convicted of a felony. The company is a T Shirt manufacturer, named Big Jim's Tees and the position would be loading and unloading trucks. Thomas nervously hands the application to the owner of the company, Big Jim. Big Jim is a large older black man in his early sixties that wears overalls, thick rimmed glasses with a head full of long gray hair. After reading over his application and following a very brief interview, Big Jim says to Thomas, "Is everything on this application true and can you pass a drug test?" A stuttering Thomas says, "Yes sir and yes sir." Big Jim then asks, "So if you get hired, when could you start?" An excited Thomas says, "I can start as early as right now if you need me to. I need to be working as soon as possible." Big Jim says, "Well, guess I will see you tomorrow then. Do whatever you have to do to pass a drug test." Thomas says, "So, I got the job? Mane I could hug you." Big Jim says, "Now all that won't be necessary son. You hug me and I might change my mind about hiring you. Now read over this and sign it." He hands Thomas the paperwork, which includes the company handbook, that an anxious Thomas signs without reading any of it. Thomas checks the time and sees that his bus is about to come in ten minutes. He tells Big Jim, "Thank you sir, but I gotta roll, I will see you tomorrow bright and early." He runs through downtown and makes it to the bus stop just in time to catch the bus. Excited about his new job, he smiles the entire bus ride home. During the bus ride he maps out getting an apartment and a car in a month's time. As soon as he enters the halfway house, Thomas immediately calls his probation officer to tell him the good news that he's found a job.

The following morning, Thomas is up bright and early at 5 am although he doesn't have to be at work until 8 am. He paces the floor anxiously awaiting the time for him to head to the bus stop. He arrives at work at 7 am much to the surprise of Big Jim who says to him, "You know your shift don't start for another hour. You can start working but this hour will be on the house." Thomas replies," Man I just wanted to make sure I got here on time since I haven't worked in a long time due to the car accident I was injured in." Thomas explains the gaps in his work history to Big Jim by saying he was in a car accident years ago that left him unable to work. That is one of the reasons why Big Jim hires him. Thomas immediately starts working. His first day he spends it shadowing an older guy named Cliff. Cliff has been working there for over ten years and he has nothing but good things to say about the company. When not shadowing Cliff, Thomas unloads supplies from trucks and boxes up shirts to prepare them for shipping. Before he realizes it, it's 1 pm and Cliff comes over to get him to tell him that it's time to take a lunch break. Cliff offers Thomas some of the spaghetti and cornbread that his wife made him for lunch. A hungry Thomas quickly accepts the offer, so he doesn't have to spend any money on lunch. During the break him and Cliff have long conversations about sports and just life in general during which time Thomas scarfs down lunch in five minutes. Noticing how fast Thomas ate his food, Cliff asks, "So how long were you in for?' A surprised Thomas says, "In what, the Army?" Cliff says, "No, in prison youngblood? I can tell. I don't buy that BS car wreck story. It's no big deal. I did a little prison time myself." Thomas says, "Mane chill out, I ain't been to no prison." Cliff says, "Ok, it's all good youngblood." Cliff then lets Thomas know that if he got his forklift driving license, he could make up to twenty-five dollars an hour. An excited Thomas quickly replies, "And how can I start that process? I'm trying to get paid." Cliff tells him he will get that info to him tomorrow. Once the break is over, Thomas heads back over to complete his tasks for the day which consists of taking shirts off the press, loading them into boxes and putting them on the truck for shipping. Once 5 o'clock hits, Cliff has to come over to tell Thomas it's time to quit for the day. Thomas says, "But man I'm not done with this last order." Cliff says, "Man that stuff will be here tomorrow and plus Big Jim not paying no overtime." Thomas packs up his things and strolls to the bus stop to head back to the halfway house. The bus doesn't come until 6 pm so he enjoys the downtown sites on his

way to the bus stop. Nothing is the way he remembers them.
Most of the small shops and restaurants have been replaced with
large stores and chain restaurants. After visiting a few stores just
to pass time, Thomas heads to the bus stop. The bus arrives, he
boards, pays his fare and takes a seat on the back of the bus. As
soon as he takes his seat, he immediately falls asleep. Waking up
so early, the hard work and overall excitement of the day finally
catches up to him. Thomas sleeps the entire forty-five-minute
bus ride, and the bus driver has to come to the back of the bus to
wake him up to let him know when he's reached his stop.

Every weekday for the next two weeks Thomas follows
the same routine, up at 5 am daily for work and he spends the
weekends reading IT blogs and working on a computer he is
building. The day he has been waiting on has finally come,
payday. He's at work bright and early as usual. His day goes as
it usually goes, except since it's payday he actually treats himself
to lunch. He goes to a Soul Food place a few blocks away from
his job. He talks to his waitress most of the time without hardly
even eating anything. Before he knows it, his lunch break is over,
and he is going to be late getting back to work. He asks for a to
go box and the waitresses' number, which she gives him both,
before he rushes back to work. He runs in and clocks in and gets
back to work. As the workday comes to an end, Big Jim tells
Thomas to come see him in his office. Thomas stops what he is

doing and runs up the steps leading to Big Jim's office. Expecting to get his paycheck, he walks in and laughs and says, "I knew you would give me my paycheck at the end of the day but trust I'm not mad about that at all. You probably thought I would all of a sudden get sick and have to leave early today once I got my hands on that check." Big Jim doesn't laugh and says," Son take a seat." Thomas slowly sits down and says," What's going on? If this is about me returning from lunch late today, I can make that up on Monday." Big Jim says, "This ain't about them damn ten minutes. This is about you lying to me son. Your background check came back, and it explains why you haven't worked in years. Your ass was in the penitentiary." Thomas says, "I can explain why I lied. Every spot I went to turned me down when I told the truth. I just want a fair chance and you gave me one." Big Jim cuts him off and says, "Yeah, yeah, yeah. That sounds good, but I still have to let you go." Thomas jumps up and says, "Come on man. This is some bullshit. I bust my ass every day here for you, and this is the thanks I get. Cliff has done time too and he's still working here." Big Jim stands up and says, "First of all, didn't you learn about not snitching in the big house and second of all, Cliff is one of my good childhood friends and he didn't go to jail for robbing and shooting some random tax paying citizen, that happens to be my first cousin, like your trifling ass did. You lucky I don't put my foot in your ass. Now get the hell out of my office." Thomas screams, "I didn't do any of that stuff mane, but you wouldn't believe it if I told you what really happened. But it's all good though. But where is my damn paycheck? Let me get that so I can roll." Big Jim laughs and says, "Boy get out of here. I don't have a check for you. Just use the two weeks you worked here as experience to make your resume look good. If they call, I will be sure to give you a glowing review. I will leave off the fact that you are a thieving liar." Thomas yells back," If I don't get my check there is gonna be a big problem." Big Jim says, "If you don't leave there is gonna be an even bigger problem for you, I'm gonna call the police. Sue me to get your check and you might get those seven hundred dollars sometime next year after you pay thousands in court costs to get it." After the threat of calling the police, Thomas decides it's in his best interest to just leave. He says goodbye to Cliff and the rest of the crew on his way out.

An angry Thomas heads to the bus stop cussing and screaming. He kicks over a couple of trashcans along the way. He sits at the bus stop for an hour plotting on how he can get his money from Big Jim. He considers waiting on him outside the building and robbing him. Knowing that robbing Big Jim will get him sent right back to jail, that thought quickly leaves his mind. When the bus finally arrives, Thomas pays his fare and walks slowly to the back of the bus to find a seat. Thirty minutes into the bus ride, Thomas pushes the button to notify the driver that he wants to get off at the next stop. Thomas decides that he is going to take a longer walk back to the halfway house so he can clear his head and think about what his next move will be. During his walk home he decides to stop by a corner store to get a drink and some chips. He goes into the store and stops and looks around because there are boxes and trash everywhere. There is a young Indian man behind the counter that immediately begins watching Thomas closely. Thomas grabs the chips and a drink and heads to the register. He says to the young man, "Y'all need some help? I can help keep this place straight for y'all. It's a mess in here." The young man ignores Thomas as he tries to figure out how to scan his items. He eventually just types the prices of the items in. Thomas then says, "Man I can help you with that register too. Won't even charge you too much for it. I know all about Point-of-Sale Systems. No way you should be manually entering items and typing in prices with this new system that you have. I can hook that up to where all of the items are just in there and all you would have to do is scan them." The cashier says, "Whateva my nigga, your total is three dollars." Thomas asks, "What did you just say mane? I should whoop your smart mouth ass." The cashier responds by saying, "You heard me my nigga. Now get out of here with your BS lies. You probably just want me to let you back here so you can steal

the register or something." The cashier closes the register and
tells Thomas he can have the items and to just leave before he
calls the police. Thomas says, "Ain't nobody about to steal from
your punk ass store." He knocks over a rack of chips before
storming out the store. After the encounter at the store, Thomas
grows even more angry and frustrated and he is thinking more
and more about getting revenge on Big Jim. He walks a few
blocks from the convenience store and eventually ends up at
Troy's. He decides to go inside to get a sandwich and to chill out
for a minute. Troy walks over to him and asks if he can take his
order. Thomas says, "Let me get a fish sandwich with mustard
only, an order of fries and a Coke." Troy says, "Ok gotcha, it will
be ready in about fifteen minutes." As Troy walks away Thomas
stops him and asks, "Are you hiring? Man, I need a job bad as
hell." Troy says, "Sorry, but I'm not hiring at the moment. Hey
man I remember you. You got locked up messing with that fool
Trey back in the day. I ain't seen you in a while. You just getting
home?" Thomas says, "Yeah man, that's me. That dummy that
did all that time for something he didn't do." Troy says,
"Welcome home. You got a second chance out here, so make the
best of it. Just make sure you stay away from that fool Trey."

Thomas eats his food and walks out of the restaurant to
head back to the halfway house. As he walks out the door, he
bumps into a man who immediately says to Thomas, "Watch

where the hell you are going." Thomas just stares at the man without saying a word before the man says, "Thomas, is that you?" The man he bumps into is Trey. "What's good man? How long you been out?" An angry Thomas says, "So you just gonna stand there and pretend like you not the reason I was locked up for all those years? Are you crazy?" Trey says, "Look mane I can't change what happened in the past, but I definitely got you going forward. I ain't got no bread on me right now but I gotcha in a couple of weeks. I might have a job for you. I could use some muscle." Thomas says, "Whatever mane. Save the lies. It's not like you to not be out here making money and I'm definitely not working for you. I tell you what though, let me get that pistol in your waist band and we can call it even." Trey reaches in his waistband, pulls out the gun and hands it to Thomas and asks, "What you about to do with it?" Thomas laughs and says, "Now why would I tell your rat ass anything about what I'm about to do?" As he walks away Thomas says to the kids that Trey has working for him, "Watch this rat bastard, he will get you sent to jail in a heartbeat." Thomas decides that he is going to go back to the store to scare the smart mouth clerk. Thomas walks the few blocks back to the store. As he approaches, he puts his hood on his head and hypes himself up to go in the store. Noticing Terry in the store, he walks around to the side of the building to wait until he leaves. As Terry leaves

Chapter 3 – Can't Teach An Old Dog New Tricks?

the store, Thomas comes from around the side of the building. He watches as Terry hurries to the car and right before he enters the store Terry looks back and calls his name. This is when Terry approaches him and attempts to talk him out of going into the store. After watching Terry pull off, Thomas puts the phone Terry gave him in his hoodie's pocket and goes back to the side of the building and puts the gun in the dumpster. Although he hides it from Terry, he is ecstatic about the job opportunity, so he immediately calls Terry. When Terry answers Thomas says, "So celly, does that job offer still stand?" Terry responds, "Hell yeah man. Come see me tomorrow morning at the address on my business card so you can fill out the paperwork." Thomas says, "Thanks man, I will not disappoint you. See you tomorrow boss." Both Thomas and Terry hang up. Thomas is ecstatic and plans on being at Terry's office first thing in the morning, but those plans are quickly derailed. While he and Terry were out front talking, the clerk recognized Thomas from earlier and thinking he was coming back to harm him, he calls the police. So as Thomas comes from beside the building, he is greeted by two officers with their guns drawn yelling "Freeze, take your hands out your pockets and put them above your head."

Chapter 4
It's A Small World After All

As JR is laying on the ground waiting to be cuffed, one of the officers gets a call on the radio. The police dispatch says, "Officer Jones, what is your location? There is a potential armed robbery about to take place at the K&J Market on 4th and South Anderson Street. You still in the area?" Officer Jones responds by saying, "Yeah but I'm kind of in the middle of something here." The other officer, Officer Schwartz, reaches over and grabs his radio and says, "We are on the way." He says to Officer Jones, "Let the kid go. We got Trey's dirty ass already." Officer Jones says, "Well today is your lucky day kid. I guess my partner is in a forgiving mood today. But I'm pretty sure I will catch you later. Enjoy the rest of your evening." As the officers run to their car, JR gets up off the ground and immediately takes off running. He runs for about five minutes before hearing sirens and seeing police cars fly pass him. Once JR makes it to the front steps of his building, he hears over twenty-gun shots in the distance. He freezes momentarily before running up the sixteen flights of stairs to his apartment where Lil E is waiting for him. He frantically opens the door, enters the apartment, and slams the door behind him. He sits on the floor breathing heavily with his back against the door. He and Lil E remain in their apartment for the remainder of the night.

As the officers drive the three blocks to the store, they get a call with the description of the robbery suspect. He's a black male, about six foot and two inches tall, weighing approximately two hundred and forty pounds wearing a black hoodie, black jeans and black tennis shoes. According to the caller, the suspect is waiting outside of the store and possibly has a gun. When the officers pull into the parking lot of the store, they see a man fitting the description of the suspect coming from the side of the building. The man they see is Thomas. The officers jump out of the car and scream," Freeze! Take your hands out of your pockets and put them above your head!" Thomas quickly removes his hands from his hoodie pockets with the cellphone that Terry gave him still in his left hand. The officers scream," Gun!" and immediately fire several shots at the unarmed Thomas. As Thomas falls to the ground, the cellphone he is holding falls out of his hand. One of the officers, Officer Schwartz, slowly approaches Thomas and rolls him over onto his stomach and cuffs him. Officer Jones then runs over to pick up what he thinks is the gun which turns out to just be a cellphone. He says to Officer Schwartz, "Get over here, I think we've messed up big time. It's a damn cellphone." People from the neighborhood start approaching, cussing and screaming at the officers. Officer Jones immediately goes into the store to ask the cashier to give him the recording from the store's cameras while Officer Schwartz just stays outside pacing back and forth. Officer Jones comes out of the store carrying the store's DVR and yells at

Chapter 4 – It's A Small World After All

Officer Schwartz," What the hell are you doing? Get these people under control. Get your head in the damn game. Here, just take this to the car." Officer Jones hands Officer Schwartz the DVR and then goes to the side of the building to look around. Officer Jones is a crooked cop that normally carries a throw away pistol and drugs that he occasionally plants on unsuspecting people to make an arrest. On this particular day though, he doesn't have the pistol with him so he's hoping to find any weapon on the side of the building. In the past he's found weapons hidden by the dumpster and today is his lucky day. While looking through the dumpster, Officer Jones sees the gun that Thomas had earlier. Officer Jones reaches into the dumpster and pulls the gun out and places it in his back pocket. He then proceeds to tell all the onlookers to back away or they will be arrested. He calls Officer Schwartz over and says, "Look, I just found a gun over in that dumpster. What I need is for you to distract these people while I slide this gun under him. You got it?" Officer Schwartz turns around and immediately pulls out his pepper spray and his gun while screaming at the crowd, "Everyone back the hell up before I shoot. Back up now!" As Office Schwartz distracts the crowd, Officer Jones slips the gun from his back pocket and while kneeling down to pretend to check Thomas' pulse, he slides the gun under Thomas' body. As he is sliding the gun under Thomas, the phone Terry gave Thomas rings and Officer Jones quickly grabs it to silence the ringer and places the phone in his pocket. One of the onlookers says, "I see what you just did you dirty pig. That boy ain't have nothing but a damn cellphone." Finally, other officers arrive on the scene along with the ambulance followed by several news crews. The EMTs jump out of the ambulance and screams to the officers, "Why is this man handcuffed? Uncuff him now!" The officers immediately remove the handcuffs from Thomas' wrists and the EMTs begin performing CPR on him. Thomas is severely injured, but he still has a pulse, so the EMTs get the stretcher out and load him into the ambulance and speed off. Unfortunately, though, Thomas succumbs to the ten gunshot wounds while en route to the hospital. Upon receiving the news that Thomas has died, more and more people in the neighborhood begin to gather around the store where the shooting takes place. Officers at the scene eventually disperse tear gas into the crowd which leads to the crowd becoming violent. Bricks and bottles are thrown through the windows of the store. Officers shoot rubber bullets in the crowd injuring several people. The crowd eventually makes their way into the store and proceeds to attack the clerk that called the police. The crowd manages to drag the clerk outside and then set the store on fire. This isn't the first time an incident like this has taken place at this convenience store. Less than a year earlier, the same clerk shot and killed a twelve-year-old kid after accusing him of shoplifting and was cleared of all of the charges, so there has always been tension between the owners of the store and the people in the community. In the end, over thirty people are injured in the melee, including five police officers and ten arrests are made.

　　After the phone conversation with Thomas, Terry continues to drive around for a little over an hour and a half before finally deciding to head home. He calls Thomas one more time during his hour-long drive to remind him to be at his office in the morning, but his call goes unanswered. He finally makes it home, parks and gets out the car and heads into the house. He walks into the house and is greeted by MiMi. He kneels down and pets MiMi on the head and yells to Stacy, "Baby you will not believe the crazy day I've had." He gets no response, so he says, "Baby, where are you?" Stacy continues to not respond, so Terry rushes upstairs and walks into their bedroom where he finds Stacy sitting on the edge of their bed crying while looking at the television. Terry says, "Pumpkin, what's going on baby? Come on now baby, it's going to be ok." Stacy is often depressed because they have been trying to have a child for a couple of years now unsuccessfully, and Stacy recently found out that it is due to her not being able to have kids, so Terry assumes that is what's bothering her. Stacy continues to cry and just points to the television. On the television is the police chief outside of the convenience store giving a press conference regarding the shooting death of Thomas. The police chief states, "My officers acted in self-defense, and I feel once the evidence is reviewed, my officers will be cleared on any and all charges that may be brought against them. Mr. Thomas Robinson, a convicted felon with a lengthy criminal record, posed an immediate threat to my officers. When asked to comply, Mr. Robinson brandished a firearm, and my officers were forced to fire several shots to subdue the suspect who had been waiting outside the store preparing to rob the location. According to the clerk, he and Mr. Robinson had an altercation a few minutes earlier and we think he was returning for revenge." They show a picture of Thomas on the screen once he finishes the press conference and Terry screams, "That's my boy! I was just at that store with him talking him out of doing some BS. I know he did not go through with that. I just offered him a job and he said he would come by the office in the morning to see me." A crying Stacy says, "That's my older cousin." Terry says, "Are you serious? He was my cellmate when I was in juvenile. He was locked up for something he didn't even do. I'm so sorry Pumpkin." He hugs her tight as she cries uncontrollably. He asks, why have you never mentioned him? Were you guys very close growing up?" She steps away and says, "Yes, we were close when we were younger, before he went to jail, but that's not all that's going on with my family. Terry says, "What else is going on?" As she starts to answer, she just points to the television again. An update to an earlier story is being reported. The news reporter says, "In a bizarre twist to a story that we reported earlier, the young woman that was found slain this morning has been identified as the younger sister of Thomas Robinson, the man that was shot and killed during a confrontation with the police. Teresa Tonechia Robinson was found by sanitation workers early this morning in an alley." The news then shows Teresa's picture and Thomas says, "Pumpkin, that's the prostitute that I was telling you about earlier." Stacy screams, "My cousin wasn't a damn prostitute. I don't care what you think you saw. I can't believe this. I literally just bonded her out yesterday and gave her a ride home." Terry hugs Stacy tight as she cries. Several minutes pass and Stacy pushes Terry away and says, "Damn, we have to go." She grabs her keys and jacket and runs out the door as Terry runs behind her yelling, "Where are we going?" They jump in the car; Stacy throws the car in reverse, and they head out the driveway and up the street and out of their subdivision. They drive thirty minutes in total silence as Stacy weaves in and out of traffic. She finally stops at an apartment building, and she jumps out quickly and tells Terry to hurry up. They run into the lobby of the building and head to the elevators. After waiting five minutes she runs to the stairwell and Terry follows behind

her. After running up several flights of stairs they get off on the
sixteenth floor and run down the hall until they get to apartment
1629. She catches her breath, then gently knocks on the door. A
child in the apartment says, "Who is it?" Stacy says, "It's your
cousin Stacy. You've probably heard your mom talk about me
and call me Pumpkin. Your mom is Tee Tee?" The kid finally
cracks the door with the chain still latched and says, "Yeah
what's up?" Stacy asks, "Can we come in?" He responds by
saying, "We?" Stacy says, "Yes, me and my husband, Terry."
Terry steps over so the kid can see him and to his surprise it's the
kid from Troy's, JR. They both look at each other startled so
Stacy asks, "Do you two know each other?" Both Terry and JR
quickly respond no. JR opens the door and lets them in. He says
to Stacy, "Where is my mom?" Stacy says, "That is why I am
here. Can you please sit down for a second?" JR sits down on
the couch and Stacy sits in between him and Lil E. She starts
crying and puts her arm around both them and says," I have
something to tell you all. This isn't going to be easy, but your
mother passed away this morning." JR jumps up and screams
"What do you mean she passed away?" Stacy continues to cry
and can barely get out a sentence, so Terry says, "I'm sorry lil
man, but her body was found early this morning. She was
murdered." JR screams, "I know Big E did this. I swear I am
going to kill him." Terry says, "Who is this Big E?" A sobbing JR

says, "He's my little brother's dad. He's in jail now for killing someone else." JR, Lil E and Stacy all cry uncontrollably for the next ten minutes while Terry tries his best to console them all. As he holds back tears, Terry then says to the boys, "Pack a bag, y'all are coming with us tonight. Man, y'all don't need to be alone tonight." Stacy gets up and hugs Terry tightly as the boys gather their belongings.

They all get into the car and Terry drives off to head home. On the ride home they stop and get hamburgers and fries from a local spot. As they head home Lil E, and JR immediately open their food and begin to eat. With a mouth full of fries JR says, "Hey, can we see her? Lil E says, "Yeah, I want to see my mom." Stacy looks over at Terry and she tells him to call the morgue so they can view the body. Terry thinks it's a very bad idea, but Stacy tries to convince him that they need to see her. Terry pulls the car over and asks Stacy to get out. He says, "Baby, we need to think about this. You don't know what happened to her or what she may look like right now. We need to get them home." Stacy finally comes to her senses and agrees that having the boys see her may be too much for them. Terry and Stacy both get back in the car and tell the boys that they cannot see their mom tonight and that they would have to wait until the viewing to see her. The boys cry about it, but in the end JR understands why. As Terry pulls into their subdivision, they see police cars and officers all over the streets. As Terry rides by, he says to one of the officers, "Hey, what's going on?" The officer says, "One of your neighbors is barricaded in his home. He's wanted for the murder of a young lady that was found slain early this morning." Terry whispers to Stacy, "I saw Mr. Charles this morning right after talking to your cousin. I wouldn't be surprised if it was him. This is crazy. I never trusted that weirdo anyway." When they get in the house, they turn on the news and what Terry believes is true; they are reporting that Charles Willingham, is not only responsible for Teresa's murder, but they suspect that he is responsible for the murders of five other women who were murdered over a twenty-year period. Charles Willingham was just one of the many aliases that he has used over the years. He is eventually convicted of all the murders and sentenced to death.

A few months pass, and the trial for the officers involved in the shooting death of Thomas finally begins, with the main piece of evidence being the video of Thomas being shot and killed. The surveillance footage from the convenience store was retrieved before Officers Jones and Schwartz got a chance to remove it from the scene and it clearly shows that Thomas was shot with his hands in the air while holding nothing but a cellphone. During opening arguments, the Prosecution describes Officer Jones and Officer Schwartz as rogue police officers with a

long history of abuse and corruption. The Defense describes
Thomas as a violent career criminal that went back to the store
seeking revenge for the earlier altercation with the clerk and that
the officers were actually heroes for shooting him. The trial is
followed closely across the United States as there are several
major news outlets present in the courtroom on a daily basis. The
national media provides up to the minute trial coverage on all of
their networks that keep the nation engulfed in the trial. Finally,
after several weeks of back and forth with hundreds of witnesses'
testimony, one of whom was Terry, the Defense and Prosecution
give their closing arguments and await the jury's decision. After
two days of deliberation, the jury finally comes back with the
verdict. As everyone in the courtroom is asked to stand by the
bailiff, the Judge says," Madam Forewoman, on count one, of
murder in the first degree, how does the jury find the
defendants?" She says, "We the jury find the defendants not
guilty of murder in the first degree." There are loud outbursts
from supporters on both sides and several people are forced to
leave the courtroom. Once the courtroom chatter dies down, the
judge says, "Madam Forewoman, on count two, of murder in the
second degree, how does the jury find the defendants? She says,
"We the jury find the defendants not guilty of murder in the
second degree." Once again, the courtroom erupts, and several
people have to be restrained and are escorted from the courtroom

in handcuffs.   In the end, the officers are found not guilty on all of the more serious charges. They are only found guilty on the lesser charges, which are obstruction of justice and tampering with evidence, which both stem from the officers attempting to remove the DVR from the crime scene. Since the DVR had been disconnected by Officer Jones, there was no footage of Officer Jones actually placing the gun under Thomas' body. Coupled with the fact that Thomas' fingerprints were found on the weapon, the jury believes that Thomas had a gun on him during the shooting, which in their opinion made the shooting justifiable.

After the not guilty verdict is returned, riots that last for several weeks ensue. Buildings are burned and protests take place outside of the courthouse as well as outside of police precincts throughout the city. Once the riots are over, millions of dollars in damages are incurred, several hundreds of arrests are made, and multiple people sustain critical injuries. The only punishment for the officers involved in the shooting, Officers Jones and Schwartz, is desk duty for a year. To add insult to injury, once reinstated, Officers Jones and Schwartz are reassigned to patrol the same neighborhood where they shot and killed Thomas.

A prominent civil rights attorney eventually comes to town and becomes involved, and a civil suit is filed on behalf of the family. After a few months of litigation, the city awards the closest living relatives of Thomas, who are Eric Anderson Jr. (Lil E) and Jesse Robinson (JR), who have both since been officially adopted by Terry and Stacy, with a fifty-million-dollar wrongful death settlement. Using an idea that JR came up with, they use the majority of the money to renovate an old area in the neighborhood that contains several old and abandoned factories and converts them into a Business Park named, The Teresa Robinson Business Park, after his mother. The Teresa Robinson Business Park contains a recreational center that's equipped with a basketball court, a workout facility and a swimming pool, a day care that provides free childcare for women in the community, an automotive repair shop that also provides auto diesel training to anyone in the neighborhood, a barber shop, beauty salon and nail shop along with a beauty school that teaches all of the aforementioned trades, a grocery store and a factory that employs over two hundred people from the community. The Teresa Robinson Business Park is also home to The Thomas Robinson Tech Academy which teaches young adults and teenagers everything from basic computer skills to computer networking, to coding. Stacy manages the day-to-day activities of the business park and Terry eventually quits his job at DelMar Technologies as they expand the tech academy to include an IT Managed Service Provider where most of the employees are people from the community that completed courses at the Tech Academy. JR also goes on to attend a local college where he plays basketball for four years and obtains degrees in Political Science and African American Studies. Upon graduating college, JR focuses on speaking to and funding programs for at-risk youth as well as building up underserved communities throughout the city. JR and Lil E tell their Uncle Thomas' story to kids around the city letting them know the importance of not hanging out with the wrong crowd and avoiding the traps of street life. The Teresa Robinson Business Park becomes the template used by other philanthropists across the country that want to make a lasting change in the underserved communities in their cities.

Back in Hazelton United States Penitentiary, Slim, Trey and two other inmates are all in the gym exercising. Slim is on the pull up bar while Trey is bench pressing while the other two inmates spot him. Slim gets off of the pull up bar and says to Trey, "Hey short timer, how does it feel to be going home in a week?" Trey says, "It feels good OG. I'm so ready to get out of here." Slim says, "So, how did you manage to get out so soon? I thought you had at least another five years in here." Trey gets up and walks over to Slim and says, "Well between me and you OG, I had to tell them folks about some other cats that's out there doing their thing in the streets. That's part of the game, so I know you feel me. Sometimes you gotta do what you gotta do

Chapter 4 – It's A Small World After All

and anyone that gets hurt is just collateral damage. You feel me?" Slim says, "Yeah mane I feel you. Only a fool would spend any more time in this place than they have to." Trey walks back over to finish bench pressing and says to Slim, "See that's why I mess with you OG. I'm definitely gonna hold you down when I get out of here. I was skeptical at first when they transferred me to your cell for no reason. I really thought you were an informant or something." As Trey starts to bench press again, Slim laughs and says, "Well it was no coincidence that you were transferred to my cell. I know some people in high places and I'm the one that requested your transfer." As Trey tries to lift the weight again, the two inmates hold the bar against his neck. Trey says," Slim, what the hell is going on mane?" Slim responds, "You know when I told you they transferred me to this prison for disciplinary reasons? I kind of lied. I was granted a transfer here so I could be closer to my baby sister Pam and her son Randall, but you may know him as Lil Randy, or as you so eloquently put it, collateral damage." Trey pleads, "Come on mane. Don't do this bruh. I swear I didn't do nothing. Guard, do something please!" The guard on duty just turns and looks away. Slim pats Trey on the chest and says, "Relax homie, and just remember, it's all in the game. Hey guard, take me to my cell." Slim and the guard slowly exit the gym. As they make their way down the hall, Trey's muffled screams can be heard in the distance.

Made in United States
Orlando, FL
08 June 2022

18625625R00085